Philip Dale, Cyril Haviland

**Voices from Australia**

Philip Dale, Cyril Haviland

**Voices from Australia**

ISBN/EAN: 9783337311506

Printed in Europe, USA, Canada, Australia, Japan

Cover: Foto ©Andreas Hilbeck / pixelio.de

More available books at **www.hansebooks.com**

# Voices from Australia

BY

PHILIP DALE

AND

CYRIL HAVILAND

London

SWAN SONNENSCHEIN & CO

PATERNOSTER SQUARE

1892

BUTLER & TANNER,
THE SELWOOD PRINTING WORKS,
FROME, AND LONDON.

# CONTENTS.

---

## Part I. Poems by Philip Dale.

# Part II. Poems by Cyril Habiland.

# PART I.

## Poems

BY

PHILIP DALE

B

# DOROTHY : A MEMORY.

## CANTO I.

IN a village where the roses make the soft air sweet
and faint,

Lived alone two orphan sisters, in a cottage small
and quaint :

One a tall and stately woman, with a mother's
tender air ;

One a winsome little maiden, with a face surpassing fair,

Like an apple's snowy blossom, as it newly drifteth
down,

E'er the contact with the dark earth shall have
made it sere and brown—

3

E'er the winds, like Earth's wild passions, shall
    have torn its leaves apart —

Torn and withered all its petals, broken like the
    human heart.

Thus it is the purest emblem of a maiden's gentle
    life,

E'er she change from child to woman, and become
    a faithful wife.


And that noble, fair-faced woman loved that little
    sister well,

With the strong and true devotion that no time can
    ever quell ;

As at first she took a baby from a senseless
    mother's breast,

Took it in the deepest sorrow, laid it on her own
    to rest ;

Took it from Death's heavy hand clasp, took it
 with a mother's prayer,
With a girlish, sweet ambition it should have a
 mother's care—
And the years, so swiftly sweeping, from that girl
 had taken youth,
Leaving with her, more than beauty, a resolve
 fulfilled with truth.


There was such a perfect calmness in her lovely
 restful eyes,
That reflected back the glory of a faith that never
 dies ;
And that mother, now an angel, gazed upon that
 little child,
With contentment of a mother, gazed again and
 sweetly smiled.

Margaret, looking on the starlight, ponders on that
home above,—

" Mother, I have kept my promise ; Dorothy has
all my love."


Now the evening time is creeping, casting shadows
on the grass—

Shadowy lights that grow and lengthen as the
happy sunbeams pass

To that home beyond the cloud-line where the sky
and waters meet,

And the evening breeze awakens balmy perfumes
soft and sweet,

And the mignonette is creeping, like the ghost of
other years,

And the stars, so brightly peeping, now are blotted
out with tears.

Little Dorothy is weaving lovely chains of visions
  bright,

Blending, in that woof of glory, all the radiant
  evening light ;

Building castles that the sunshine never leaves by
  night or day,

Wrapping all with wildest heart-hopes, which,
  alas ! must fade away.

And her hair had caught a radiance e'er the
  sunlight went to rest,

Painting gold and crimson pictures, as it swept the
  cloudy west ;

Standing backward from the battle, with her free
  untroubled heart—

Knowest, dreaming little maiden, thou must one
  day take thy part ?

Know that man was ne'er intended to rest calmly
  in this world—

Not to kings were banners given, that they might
be always furled.


Dorothy is vaguely dreaming of a Prince that is to
come,

Flaming out with many colours, heralded with
spear and drum.

Clad in all the costliest raiment, with a face of
beauty rare,

And the shades of night would whiten, laid against
his ebon hair.

And this Prince would kneel before her, pleading
for her precious smile ;

She would answer, coyly, shyly, with each lovely
maiden wile.

All the deepening, gloating shadows, all the leaves
that rustle by,

By her fancy are unheeded, never catch her
dreaming eye.

Margaret's voice comes breaking softly on the
fairy, spell-bound scene :

"Truant maiden ! little blossom ! child, you know
you must not dream,—

Dreaming of a perfect future brings my dear one
only pain ;

Promise, Dorothy, my baby, thou wilt never dream
again,

For, alas ! to-morrow's sunlight bears my little
child away ;

And this evening, sweet, has ended all our lovely
holiday.

Schoolmates, dear, give welcome gladly to the
friend they love so well ;

I resign thee, dear, for duty—none my loneliness
can tell,

And I press upon you, darling, to be happy while
    you may ;

Youth was made for love and sunshine—shadows
    come with later day.

Do not dream of lovers, blossom ; bind thy hopes
    upon my heart ;

Dorothy, my child, my mission, I can never from
    thee part :

Thou hast beauty, thou mayst hear it better from
    a sister's tongue ;

Do not let it change thee, darling,—thou art very,
    very young.

Now come to my feet, my sunbeam, rest thy head
    against my knees ;

Let thy hair, like golden ripples, answer to the
    evening breeze ;

Tell me of thy little sorrows, let me share each
    childish joy,

Let me regulate them, darling, so that time may

    not destroy

All thy hopes, like sickled barley, leaving only

    withered blades ;

I will smile upon thy sunshine, strive to brighten

    all its shades.

Listen, baby ! I have sworn it, I will shield thee

    with my love.

Look ! the stars are peeping, sweet one,—'tis our

    mother's eyes above.

I have never loved save thee, dear, now of course

    I never will ;

Had I long since loved and wedded, thou hadst

    been the first one still.

Dorothy, the moon is rising brightly o'er yon

    distant hill,

Little birds have gone to rest, dear ; all the world

    seems hushed and still ;

And my bird must gain her nest too.   Let me
    bless her e'er she goes,

I will guard thy life, my darling ; I will keep thee
    from all woes ;

Not by efforts unassisted.   Let us pray to God in
    heaven—

For through Him descend our blessings, and
    through Him are mercies given."

E'en as Jacob craved for blessing, kneeling at his
    father's side,

Dorothy knelt before her sister, and the moonlight
    flooded wide,

Far across that sacred picture, wrapping them in
    hallowed light,

Dimming all the crimson roses, robing all in
    softest white.

## CANTO II.

Days and weeks have vanished quickly, taking
  Dorothy on their wing —

Margaret waiting, lonely, patient, for the time she
  knows will bring

Back again her golden sunbeam, who will gladden
  with her song,

Who will laugh and make glad music, when the
  time seems lone or long.

But the future—how mysterious ! Could she tell
  what it would bring ?

She would love another's footsteps, she would hear
  another sing ;

With another she would wander in the garden,
  'neath the moon,

And her heart, at length awakened, sweetly then
would beat to tune.

She would grow to watch the changes on another
much-loved face,

All the shadows marked by sorrow she would
gladly learn to trace.

Dorothy she had chid for dreaming, now her life
she dreamed away,

And the harp so long unfingered, echoed to the
sweetest lay;

It was love, the crowning blessing of a lonely
woman's life :

She had made a perfect sister, she would make a
perfect wife.

And the Prince who waked this passion, was he
like her girlish dreams ?

Was he fair, this man who brightened all her life
with radiant gleams ?

See, he leans against the casement, which was

    Dorothy's chosen place,

And the sunbeams lighten gently o'er his rugged,

    careworn face.

As his eyes are deep with sorrow, so his hair is

    tinged with grey ;

But a charm lies on his features that no time can

    take away.

Is it in the saddest sweetness of the smile that

    lights his face ?

Is it in his every movement, waking still unstudied

    grace ?

We may surely ne'er define it ; still, it rests in

    beauty there,

Defying all that time may ravish, lighting up the

    grey blent hair.

And this man who, tired and weary of the world's

    exceeding care,

Came to ponder well and deeply, saw and loved
    this woman fair—

Not with passion did he sue her,—that belongs of
    right to youth ;

He had long since spent its splendour, he had
    tasted bitter Truth,

How the joys we clasp in gladness, never shading
    with our fears,

Fade and go like dimmest phantoms till we soften
    them with tears—

And this woman, calm and restful, came like balm
    upon his soul,

And he gave her all the reverence taken from the
    vanished whole.

E'en as water freshens violets, taking up the
    bended flowers,

So he learned to turn to Margaret in the lovely
    summer hours ;

As the tired deer flies to shelter from the burning

    noontide sun,

As the traveller resteth gladly when his weary work

    is done,

So he learned to rest on Margaret, as a nobler,

    statelier thing ;

He had done with love and passion,—peace was

    all his life could bring.


Thus it was, while he awakened all the love within

    her breast,

She was only healing sorrows, giving to the weary

    rest,

And she listened to his mourning, till his burden

    seemed to fade ;

Thus there came a sunshine, springing slowly,

    surely through the shade.

"Margaret," he would cry at evening, resting
  calmly at her feet,
"Have the angels spoken to thee, that thy face is
  now so sweet?
Have they cast their radiance o'er thee, taking
  from thee every care,
Lighting up thine eyes divinely, till they make thee
  wondrous fair?"



Then her face would flush with crimson, like the
  sun's fair dawning light,
And her eyes would gleam and sparkle with a
  tender, happy light—
"Denis, I would speak of Dorothy, of my little
  sister fair;
I have told you of her beauty, of her glistening
  olden hair,

And her eyes, like clouds at evening, changing to
a deeper shade,—

Happy, careless little Sunbeam, laughter-loving
little maid.

Have I told you that her nature is like water, clear
and bright,

Showing her thoughts like pebbles, Denis,
scintillating in the light ?

I have watched her life unfolding like a lovely
budding rose,

And as a child to woman merges, so a stream to
river flows ;

I have sworn to shield her always, keeping sorrow
from her brow ;

She will need us both, my Denis,—you will learn
to guard her now.

I have written to my blossom, saying, love can
ne'er destroy

All a sister's long devotion ; she must come and
    share my joy,—

She must learn to love thee, Denis ; on this thing
    my heart is set,—

Surely hope will seem abundant when the two I
    love have met.

For her life has been so cloudless, like the rising
    of the sun,

Crims'ning in the early morning all his glorious
    work begun.

We will grasp the thorns together out from where
    her feet may tread,

We will dissipate the shadows e'er they fall upon
    her head—

Ah ! I took my little blossom as a legacy from
    death ;

She was given to my keeping, with a dying
    mother's breath."

## Canto III.

Just beneath the high old fruit-trees, where the
blossoms fall like rain,

Sits a fair and graceful maiden, dreaming happy
dreams again ;

As the Alps when snowed in winter, round her
folds of drapery fair,

And the sun has stayed to glisten on her curling
golden hair,

Stayed to hallow as a picture of some mediæval
saint,

Stayed to fling the slanting sunbeams that the
artist loves to paint ;

Brush alone could give her picture, as she rests in
beauty there ;

Words, alas ! could never render half the drooping
grace so rare ;

On her lap are dewy snowdrops, and a wreath is
    on her head,
And the trees, to do her homage, half their snowy
    blossoms shed.


Margaret, in her proud exulting, placed that wreath
    upon her brow ;
" You are like a picture, darling—hush ! I hear his
    footstep now."
On he came, unheeding, calmly, all unconscious
    of his fate,
Every footstep brought him nearer, to return—
    alas ! too late ;
E'en as to the mist-blind traveller pacing down the
    mountain side,
An unconscious, heedless wanderer, to the chasm
    yawning wide.

Thus we take supremest blessings far too sure to

　　hold them fast,

And we wake in deepest mourning but to find they

　　all are past.

The future, with its sobs and gladness, well is

　　veiled from mortal eyes,

If the spring be too far distant, then the traveller

　　sinks and dies.

It is hope alone supports us, by the fears of life

　　assailed ;

Know then, 'tis the grandest ord'ring that our

　　future should be veiled.



Thus this man, careworn and weary, on this

　　peaceful summer day,

Never stopped or stayed an instant, still pursued

　　his even way ;

And the birds, who might have told him, never
    stopped his onward course ;

And the wind, which wrung the branches, never
    held him by its force ;

And the sun, who seeth all things, never cared to
    say beware ;

Thus he met a kindred spirit, thus he took another
    care.


So he saw her crowned with snowdrops like a thing
    from fairy-land,

With her eyes like saints', cast downwards, and
    some lilies in her hand ;

And he stood like one bewildered --this the thing
    he long had sought ;

In the presence of this maiden, Margaret, honour,
    all were nought.

He had thought, because world-weary, all the joys

    of life were past ;

But the love that burst upon him bound him,

    chained his heart at last.

As she raised her eyes to greet him with their

    lovely violet hue,

So his heart felt youthful freshness, such a thing to

    love and woo.


Margaret, like a stately picture, took that wreath

    from off her hair ;

" Ah ! my saint, I must uncrown thee, for I only

    placed it there

That when Denis first beheld thee, he should take

    thee for a fay ;

Now a mortal I must make thee, or perhaps thou

    may'st not stay,

But upon some golden chariot thou wilt fly to
    radiant halls,

Thou wilt fly, and happy, heedless, answer not our
    piteous calls.

See! a brother's love awaits thee—see! another
    heart is thine,

All through life, my little blossom, thou wilt have
    his care and mine."


And the days flew by like leaflets falling from an
    autumn tree,

Sowing seedlets of the sorrow that should blight
    the life of three.

And the one who would have gathered living coals
    to guard the child,

Helped the work of dire destruction, as it pros-
    pered sweetly smiled.

To this man oppressed with sorrow and by joys
   long dim and sere,

She gave all the youthful freshness of a love that
   knows no fear ;

Gave the trust that grows but once, never having
   been deceived,

In the honour of her hero, Margaret lived and still
   believed.

That her little baby sister e'er could feel a woman's
   love,

She as soon had thought the angels could have left
   their home above.

Thus fate came like snow in winter, falling lightly
   on the ground ;

In the pool that looks the stillest all the deepest
   spots are found.

In the lives that seem the staidest, half life's
   tragedies are played,

Unannounced they come, like spectres, till we wake

    afraid, dismayed.

Thus a girlish heart had wakened on that day to

    grief and pain,

Never idly in the sunshine would she dream her

    dreams again- -

Never take life's web of tangles from the place she

    laid it down,

All the roseate glorious colours now, alas! were

    tinged with brown.

———

For one evening when the rain-drops culled the

    sweetness of the flowers,

And the birds drank in the freshness from their

    nests beneath the bowers,

And the twilight hour was deep'ning, robbing

    shadows from the sky,

And while love was idly steeping all the hours that

fleeted by ;

Thus the hour evoked the story, which is new, and

yet so old—

As a shower draweth perfumes from the sun-dried,

scented mould.

" Dorothy, alas ! to see thee was to love thee,

sainted one,

As an infant loves its mother, as the flow'rets love

the sun.

Dorothy, I stand before thee, weary, wan, and

tired with tears,

And you, darling, stand before me in the bloom of

sixteen years.

What is there between us, dearest, but the pity in

thy heart ?

Let me tell thee all my folly, all my love before we

part ;

For to Margaret I have given all my reverence,—

'tis her due ;

Well I know her steadfast nature, well I know her

heart is true.

And she gives me pity, dear one — pity, sometimes

mixed with love—

Love that angels feel for sinners, from their happy

homes above.

She the placid, rose-decked streamlet, I the

mountain torrent, dear,—

She has ever kept to duty, like a beacon firm and

clear ;

And she feels for me compassion, such, I say, as

angels know ;

Dorothy, my flower, my fairy, tell me, darling,

must I go ? "

Then the fire of scorn exceeding flashed into her

dreaming eyes,

As the wild wind stirs the river, and its wavelets

    fall and rise.

" I, to blight my sister's lifetime—why for me this

    grievous task ?

Denis ! Denis ! let me, pray thee, think well of the

    thing you ask.

Thou wouldst bend a nature, Denis, far too pure

    to mate with thine ;

Thou wouldst break my sister's heart-hopes ; she

    would smile and give no sign.

So forget the words just uttered ; keep her love,

    for it is yours,

Keep the path of truth untarnished, and the prize

    it still ensures,

And oh ! promise she may never guess your heart

    has strayed to me ;

Keep her trust and love unshaken, and the

    brightness thou shalt see."

But he bowed his head, as young trees bend
  before the fierce wind-storm :

Anguish, love, remorse, contrition, all depicted in
  his form,

As it bent and cowered lowly, hushed before a
  sister's might,

And the trees shook down their rain-drops, making
  music in the night.


There is love that comes from passion, storming
  at the human heart ;

There is love so pure and holy, passion there can
  have no part.

There is love, as angels love us from their happy
  homes above ;

There is pity, and of all things, 'tis the sweetest
  way to love.

So it, like a whirlwind rushing, filled the maiden's
heart to-day

With a great and wondrous softness; all her pride
was swept away.

" Denis, brother, let me tell thee, I am pleading
'gainst my heart ;

Denis, Denis ! it is better you and I this day must
part.

Go to Margaret, ah ! she loves you, with a love
you now forget.

E'er you leave me, promise, Denis. Would to
God we ne'er had met !"

Then he knelt, and sued before her, in a lover's
sweetest tones,

And the wind, like Banshees wailing, sobbed
around them with its moans.

'Twas the dim, prophetic warning of the burial of
their dream ;

D

And his words flowed out before her like a
mountain's swollen stream.

"All my life is spread before thee, thine to make
or thine to mar,

Margaret is the calmer radiance of the steadfast
evening star,

All her youth is past and faded, love belongs of
right to youth,

Place your hand in mine, my darling; let us tell
her all the truth."

Once again as living craters, gleamed her eyes
against the night,

From the height of her devotion love was blotted
out of sight.

"Did I e'er confess I loved thee, did my tongue
turn traitor too?

For the heart of Margaret's sister, listen ! thou
must never sue.

I could love thee, though 'twere useless, knowing

love my life had crowned,

I could love as well and truly, though the shades

of fortune frowned,

I could love aught but a traitor, that but fills my

heart with scorn ;

Could I take thy love and wear it while my sister's

heart was torn ?

Let me then recall the utterance of a simple

childish heart ;

Love to me is like a volume bound and sealed in

every part.

I have youth, and youth has fancies, which but

stay a little while,—

In the years spread out before me I will think of

this and smile."

Then he threw her wildly from him, till she fell

against his feet

Like a crushed and lovely lily as it bends the
   earth to greet.

" Women, ah ! my long experience has but shown
   me then the truth ;

I had fancied better from thee, from thy sweet
   exceeding youth ;

All deceitful,—why should Margaret from the fatal
   taint be free ?

I have drunk the dregs, I know it ; what of life is
   left for me ?

Let me go before I scorn thee for the piteous thing
   thou art ;

Why, indeed, was beauty given, but to snare the
   human heart?

I will go ; would yonder mountains ne'er had
   frowned their heights on me !

I will break the link that binds me ; I will set thy
   sister free ! "

As he strode away, the brushwood sounded 'neath
his heavy tread,

And to Dorothy his footsteps fell upon her heart
like lead.

Gone, alas! the bloom and brightness of the past
soft summer days,

And the stars are blurred and blotted from her
yearning, tearful gaze;

As a wind across the moorland crushes down each
tender shoot,

So the awful desolation when first sorrow takes its
root,

And as when the branch is mellowed to a stately
graceful tree,

All the winds may play around it, still it standeth
firm and free;

Thus it is when time has shown us that to man
belongeth grief,

And that sorrow comes upon us swiftly as the
    falling leaf,

But at first triumphant, haughty, it has power our
    lives to chill,

As the breeze that waves the barley, Nature bends
    without a will.


So at each still fainter footfall, lower, lower bends
    her head,

And the wind that sighed around her seemed like
    masses for the dead,

And the rain fell down upon her as the angels
    wept above,

And she cried like one half stifled, " Love, ah !
    love, my love " ;

And the trees that rustled near her heard that low,
    heart-broken sigh,

And the wind caught up the echo of that last
    despairing cry,

And a night-bird singing softly 'ere he sought his
    downy nest,

Taking from the wind his message, laid it on the
    lover's breast ;

Back he rushed like one demented, raised her
    form within his arms,

As her anguish melts like sea-foam, so her sorrow
    slowly calms.


" You were brave, my simple child-love, daring for
    a sister's sake,

Such a sacrifice, my darling, as you know she
    would not take ;

All her life she has devoted to keep sorrow from
    thy path,

All the years that she has loved thee, would she
   spoil thy life at last ? "

" All my life, ah, yes, I never missed a tender
   mother's kiss ;

Must I break a heart that loves me, and return
   her care with this ?

Denis, listen ! I will never mar her life by making
   mine ;

Could I smile away from Margaret, leaving her
   alone to pine ?

Go this instant ! tell her, Denis, all the love thou
   hast for me,

Then my love will turn to hatred ; I will feel but
   scorn for thee.

If thou keep thy faith unshaken, true to her,
   whate'er the cost,

I will feel that to have known thee, life itself were
   too well lost.

Break her heart, but not to win mine, not to build

upon the ruin ;

I would shudder at the fragments of her lovely

day-dream strewn.

Denis, see, I kneel before thee, pleading for thy

mercy dear ;

'Tis thy duty to her, brother ; see thy path lies

straight and clear."


" What ! resign thee, dear, for Margaret,—fling thy

love away from me ?

Striving to make one life happy, we should wreck

the lives of three.

Three ! I ask thee what is marriage, when one

heart is stern and cold ?

Better tell her now this instant,—better, ay, a

hundred-fold."

" Denis, listen ! rest this evening ere you tell our
      Margaret all ;
Thou shalt have my answer truly ere another
      night shall fall."


" Ah ! thou givest hope, my darling.   Listen while
      I tell you, dear,
E'er another night has fallen, I must end suspense
      and fear,
For to-morrow, as the sunlight shall have tinged
      the morning sky,
As from out thy casement looking, thou shalt see
      me passing by.
All the night long, dear, consider shalt thou spoil
      three lives or one ;
Dorothy, I wait thine answer with the rising of
      the sun.

Take thy snowy kerchief, dearest, hold it where
 it meets my eye ;

If thou givest love, my treasure, hold it, Dorothy,
 on high ;

If bestowing hope and love, dear, surely then my
 life is crowned ;

If thou takest hope and life, dear, it shall flutter
 to the ground ;

For the cold earth is an emblem of our fair hopes
 doomed to die ;

But, when Fate has smiled upon us, all our hope
 must soar on high."


Thus 'twas over, and the pale moon reft the
 clouds, as though 'twould fain

Look upon the parting lovers, then she hid her
 head again,

And the breezes all had hushened till they only
seemed to sigh,

And the night alone was wakened by the curlew's
mournful cry.

E'en the rain had ceased, but glistened on each
quiv'ring grassy blade,

And the trees, at rest, were slumb'ring in their
sombre foliage shade ;

Still the flowerets gave sweet perfumes from each
trembling, dew-decked leaf,

And two hearts that night had severed —one at
least was torn with grief.

———

## Canto IV.

Dorothy sits at her casement, and the breezes cool
    her brow,

Realizing 'tis the climax, life and love, or nothing
    now,

And the past floats up before her, all the few short
    girlish years,

Marked by trifling joys and sorrows, childish
    friendship's transient tears,

They had filled her life, engrossing all her happy
    girlish heart,

Now they sank so far in distance, love had claimed
    the greater part.

Was this love bestowed for nothing? was it hers
    to fling away?

It was given as a blessing, glorifying with its
    ray;

But her sister's voice beside her fell upon her
    startled ear :

" Are you sleeping, little blossom, dreaming at
    the casement, dear ? "

And she sank down close beside her, till against
    her knee she leant,

Speaking in low, tender shyness—all her colour
    came and went —

" Dorothy, I have never spoken fully, as I speak
    to-night,

Never told you that my whole heart seems en-
    wrapped and filled with light ;

I was very lonely sometimes, till with baby lips
    you spoke,

And my life seemed sad and weary as I bended to
    the yoke ;

Then I cast such thoughts behind me ; you, my
    sister, filled my life ;

Now, indeed, has glory crowned me ; baby, I shall

    be his wife.

Sometimes when the shades of evening fall and

    nestle o'er the land,

Comes the strangest unrest o'er me that I scarce

    can understand,

For I know life is uncertain, and to him with all

    the rest ;

Dorothy, if death should claim him, it would take

    all life holds best,

For I fancy fortune never smiled so radiantly

    before.

Should I wake—oh ! no, I shudder—but to find

    my dream is o'er !

If I hear a voice upraised, dear, wild unreasoning

    though it be,

My poor heart will cease its beating, all my visions

    go from me.

See ! I am confessing, dearest, you the mentor, I
    the child ;

Mignonette, your eyes are closing, wearied with
    my fancies wild."


Truly now she seemed the mentor, grief on her
    had set its seal,

Childhood far had left behind her, she must feel
    as women feel

When they give their love unwisely, never thinking
    of the cost,

Till they wake with sad despairing, finding all they
    prized is lost.

Love can fill a life or sere it ; it has brightened
    Margaret's now,

Till she seemed the younger sister—happiness had
    smoothed her brow,

Given to her eyes a radiance that they never had
  in youth,

Never, though their light had always shone from
  out a mine of truth.

" Now I leave thee, little sunbeam ; see, the dawn
  is stealing in ;

Very soon the birds will waken, and the busy
  world begin."

So she left her happy, hopeful, never guessing at
  the fight

Dorothy had fought with duty till her very lips
  were white.

Once or twice into a lifetime comes an hour when
  hope is gone ;

Well it is it comes but seldom, or we could not
  journey on.

Dorothy, kneeling at her casement, heeds not how
  the time goes by,

Never stirring hand or muscle, seeming not to
> breathe or sigh,

And not praying—the hour is sacred to the burial
> of a love,

And the dawn comes, creeping surely, bright'ning
> all the sky above.

As Death's presence always awes us, hushing wild-
> est, loudest tread,

And respect, in life withholden, still is given to the
> dead—

So she knelt above the gravestone of long future
> happy years ;

Hope and love and youth had vanished, but she
> could not give her tears.

Kneeling like a marble statue, without breath or
> bosom shaken,

Till the sun poured forth his warning—" Maiden,
> it is time to waken."

And she heard a heavy footfall on the gravel path
below;

Then at last she raised her head up, and her eyes
were dark with woe;

From her neck she tore her kerchief, daring not to
stay or think,

Lest she falter from her purpose, fail, and perish
on love's brink,

Just an instant held it fluttering, tried to pray upon
her knees;

Then, as though she cast life from her, flung it to
the morning breeze.

For an instant it was wafted, and the birds' songs
broke the sound;

Then, as though it, too, were weary, slowly flut-
tered to the ground.

———

## CANTO V.

Hark ! the tempest loud is screaming o'er the dizzy
   mountains high ;

And the trees, like leaflets bending, as the wild
   wind rushes by ;

See the rain in streams descending, as it swells the
   water-course,

And the stalwart boughs are bending, rent and
   torn with fury's force,

And the tiny flowers are broken, short indeed
   their earthly span,

And the thunder-tone is pealing messages from
   God to man.

Lightning plays—its vivid gleaming gives to all
   things radiance bright,

Then it fades, but leaveth darker all the sable
   shades of night.

Sweet upon the tempest pealing comes the measured convent bell ;

What a sense of peace it giveth, weary hearts alone
can tell,

Ringing softly, morn and even, sending messages
of love ;

Ringing, pealing, softly dying, till the tone is
caught above.

And the bell—what is its story, as the wind around
it roars ?

Does it speak of lives devoted to a great and holy
cause,

And of charity exceeding from the Sisters of the
Cross ?

No ; it tells a sadder story of a faithful sister's loss.

———

Dorothy, the child of sunshine, born to brighten
for a time,

Then to turn her life to darkness by an act of love

    sublime—

Yes, an act by which life's future was for ever to

    her closed.

Looking downward on the battle, God Himself

    had interposed,

For life's woof, so sadly tangled, never now could

    be restored :

It had passed from human passions straight into

    the hands of God.

Now into that rose-decked village Death came

    stalking fever-cloaked,

Entering in at happy homesteads, silent, grim, and

    unprovoked,

With no warning where had echoed yesterday the

    children's shout,—

Now, where baby feet had gambolled, little forms

    were carried out,

And some mother weeping sadly o'er a little
  cherished form,

Lying there so stiff and rigid, yesterday so bright
  and warm ;

And her heart in hot rebellion cries out, "Why
  for me this grief?"

Shall we view that baby's future, shall we slowly
  turn each leaf,

Till we see a page so blotted that a mother's heart
  would break ?

God sees all,—we may not murmur; what He gave
  is His to take ;

So on Dorothy Death's shadow fell within the convent walls,

And she sank, without a struggle, as the tender
  blossom falls ;

Seeking strength to face life's future, where was
  resignation taught ?

She had lived, and almost conquered, with her
weary battle fought.

In a room, pure, sweet, and holy, sacred to the
sense of death ;

Broken by the bees' low humming, lies a girl with
failing breath.

Where the light of outside sunshine comes in
solemnly and dim,

And upon the air comes stealing sadly now the
vesper hymn ;

And two hearts, no more divided by the love they
sought to hide—

Weeping for the soul departing—life and death
stand side by side.

So the troubles which in lifetime we set up and
sadly fight,

Fade and die like empty shadows as death takes
them out of sight ;

And the life we deemed so weary, and the grief at
  which we pined,
When we look for them have vanished —Death has
  left them all behind.


Thus it was, that what in lifetime Dorothy had
  flung away,
That the act might shield a sister, Death had
  given back to-day;
And the path she had determined should have led
  them far apart,
Lo, had narrowed at the turning, till Death brought
  them heart to heart.
And she held his hand whilst turning back one
  ling'ring, wondering glance,
O'er the sad and broken pathway of her young
  life's short expanse.

Then a look into the future, lightened by mysterious grace,

Then a gaze into the yearning love and grief upon
   his face.

So, in death, she poured the story which in life she
   could not tell,

And his tears, like heart's-blood coursing on her
   cheek, in anguish fell.

For their eyes are never parted as he strains her
   to his breast,

And her face is changing slowly to a look of
   perfect rest.

Ah! the arms that round him tighten slowly,
   slowly loose their hold,

And the sun, in grief at parting, paints once more
   her hair with gold.

Then a breeze comes, bringing leaflets that an
   open rose had shed,

But too late,—no more she heeds them—little
Dorothy is dead.

And a bird had seen that parting as towards his
nest he flew,

And another entering slowly—Margaret—had seen
it too ;

Then he turned his head imploring—Dorothy
within his arms —

" Margaret, if I broke my troth-plight, Death all
anger, dear, disarms—

I will try to love thee, Margaret, for a sake now
dead and dear."

But she answered by a heart-cry mortals very
seldom hear.

Never heeding what he uttered, never hearkening
what he said—

Margaret clasped her one heart's treasure – " Leave
me, leave me with my dead ! "

Then he shrank away in silence, crushed and
    awed before this grief,

And outside the air was broken only by the falling
    leaf;

For the nuns had ceased their singing as Death's
    tidings quickly spread;

Now they stood, and scarce discovered which the
    living, which the dead;

Then they loosed, with sad tears falling, Margaret's
    clinging arms apart,

For the only sign of living was her faintly beating
    heart;

And she lay in mercy senseless, lest it strain too
    far and break:

Ah! the time when she remembers! God have pity!
    she must wake.

Then to Dorothy they tended with their gentle,
    loving hands,

Wreathing lilies on her bosom, braiding back her
  hair in bands.

This was Death, —'twas hard to think so, gazing
  on that childish face,
With its infant lines of roundness, now transfigured
  with a grace
Sent by God, and fast dispelling any lines by
  sorrow lent ;
Who could doubt when in its presence, Death
  alone by Him is sent ?

———

### Canto VI.

Outside in the deep'ning shadows lies a form
  whose anguished force
Wildly crushes tender flowerets, trying to realize his
  loss ;

Grasping at the flowers in madness, from his hand
the warm blood flowed—

Ah! remorse can know no resting, for it reaps the
grain it sowed:

Still he writhes in mutest sorrow, crushing down
his burning head;

Useless, for the wildest heart-cry cannot give us
back our dead.

This the tale the bell is striving 'midst the tempest's
force to ring,

And the nuns' sweet chant is sounding as they
softly, sadly sing,

As a form is carried past them out into the wind
and rain,

And the loud, tempestuous storming mingles with
the low refrain;

So they bear her to the hill-side over wet and
drooping flowers,

As the rain is softening gently into tender, fitful

    showers.

She who loved the glittering sunshine, was it

    weeping for her fate?

Would it shine a benediction, would it cease its

    tears too late?

E'er the grave had closed upon her, would it shed

    one gleam again?

No; for Dorothy the sunlight ever more must shine

    in vain;

So amidst the storm fast ceasing she is laid away

    at rest,

And the clouds are lightening surely in the distant

    hill-faced west,

Surely clearing, but the rain-drops still are weeping

    o'er the grave,

And as down the earth is sprinkled, comes a roll

    of sorrow's wave

From a heart that strove for calmness till that last
and awful knell;

Then a cry that burst all limits echoed out love's
sad farewell.

And the mourners, ere departing, give what
sympathy they dare

To a man whose face is rigid with a look of fixed
despair;

But he never heeds their presence, never feels the
dripping rain,

Till the earth upon her coffin bursts his grief without restrain.

As the grave is slowly filling as the last sad
mourners pass,

Denis hides his head in anguish on the wet and
sodden grass.

And to-night out in the starlight Dorothy will rest
alone;

Will she hear the deep sobs bursting from a form
    that lieth prone?

On the earth he grasps so closely that he never
    hears a tread,

Lightly falling close beside him— Margaret, too,
    has sought her dead—

Then he rises, but not speaking; 'tween them lies
    the form so dear,

That they linger, dimly conscious that they falter
    lest she hear,

And their utterance should disturb her, lying
    calmly at their feet,

As upon the air comes wafted perfumes from the
    violets sweet ;

And their fragrance breaks the silence by the
    memories they wake.

" Margaret ! Margaret ! do not leave me, do not
    spurn me, for her sake ! "

F

But she stood like some dark statue in her flowing
    mourning dress,

Gazing sadly at the sorrow he is striving to
    suppress.

" Margaret, listen ! do not blame me ; could I see
    her and not love ?

Margaret, do not thwart her wishes, do not grieve
    her now above ;

She is gazing, only hoping that our lives may
    mingle yet.

Ah ! you hold the only lightening to a life whose
    sun has set.

Margaret, see ! across our darling lies a gleam of
    watery sun ;

Ah ! thou wilt not grudge the love, dear, that
    unconsciously she won ;

For it is an omen surely that our lives must never
    part."

But she answered, coldly, sadly, " In her spring
     you broke her heart ;

In her spring you took life's glory—crushed it in
     your sinful hands.

What were you, that you should wander here, from
     distant, unknown lands,

Striding here without a warning, and with
     desolation fraught ?

Now your work is finished, view it, all the threads
     with anguish wrought ;

Why, I ask, in all the wide world, should you
     choose to tarry here,

Till you found one life quite lonely, therefore
     crushed all it held dear ? "


" Pity, Margaret—well I feel it ; I, of all men,
     should have known,

Should have passed on, dear, and left thee in thy
    peaceful, rose-decked home ;

But, ah me ! how I was tempted, none, ah, none
    could ever know,

Just to linger for a space, dear, in a vale where
    death and woe

Seemed as far off as the flowerets from the distant
    azure sky,

And the roses as they clambered, and the winds
    that rustled by

Seemed to whisper, Come and linger in this world-
    forgotten spot ;

Then a chance, a turning, Margaret—and I
    mingled with thy lot.

Often I have heard thee say it that I waked thy
    heart to life.

Ah ! no sorrow can restore her,—Margaret, wilt
    thou be my wife ?

If thy heart is sad and bleeding, I will heal with
  tender touch ;

I will make thee reparation, — for myself I ask this
  much,

That her name be buried deeply, shut out with her
  sweet-loved face.

Margaret, I will calm thy sorrow ; I will try to take
  her place."


And she answered slowly, sadly, " Denis, thou
  hast pleaded well,

All—and save the words just uttered, they a
  volume to me tell,

That thou thinkest, ah, thou thinkest thou couldst
  ever take her place,

That thy love, if it were boundless, ever, ever
  could efface

From my brain the thought that maddens, that
    I—who had gladly died,

Just that while my life still lingered she had tended
    by my side—

Should have caused her life to darken, and I ask
    you, are you free ?

No ; together we have killed her,—God in heaven
    pity me !

And you, standing there, could ask me, ask me
    e'er to smile again,

I, who in my blind self-trusting sought to shield
    her life from pain !

And how well my task succeeded we this day can
    understand ;

Denis, could I feel more keenly had I slain her
    with this hand ?

And my feelings all are frozen by an iceberg called
    Despair,

In my heart |I search now vainly, ' Dorothy ' is
written there.

And I marvel very greatly that thou ever hadst the
power

E'er to rival that dear image even for a single hour.

But 'twas so, and could the waters of the sea
obliterate

That I knew my darling's secret, and her love,
alas! too late?

Now depart, for thou hast finished all thy piteous
task of woe."

Mercy he implores before her, but she holds her
hand out—" Go."


And he rises sadly, slowly, with one last and vain
appeal :

" Margaret, is thy heart of iron? Margaret, hast
thou ceased to feel ? "

" Yes, I feel my heart is withered, stricken in its

    summer pride;

Now 'tis winter, and I know it that my better self

    has died.

Useless, useless pleading to me,—in this grave

    there lies my heart;

Rise! thy step too long has tarried; once again I

    say, Depart!"


And he rose again, but slowly, gazing backward

    as he went,

And the air around is fragrant with the earth-

    bedewèd scent;

And the sun has burst the rain-clouds, and is

    flinging o'er the grave

Of its tender little favourite one departing golden

    wave,

And on Margaret's silent figure, standing out
against the sky,

Moveless, like some grand old picture, as the
breezes rustle by.

Clasped her hands so low together, and her head
with sorrow bowed,

As the sunlight wraps and hallows round her like
a golden shroud.

Denis sees whilst still retreating, and it never
leaves his eyes ;

While he lives, it still must linger, darkening only
when he dies.

Though the sun upon the hill-tops and the fir-trees
seems to lave,

To the sight of him departing only gleams upon
that grave ;

Only on that stirless figure, till it seems enwrapped
with light,

Then he, with one long gaze backward, passed for
    ever from her sight.


\*     \*     \*     \*     \*


Thus it is from weary journeys over distant sea
    and land,

By three graves, so close together, pondering and
    sad I stand.

And I pluck the grass asunder, on which fall my
    useless tears,

Till I see in time-worn letters, " Dorothy, aged
    sixteen years."

And I feel how glad was Margaret when they laid
    her down to rest ;

At the memory of her story, sorrow rises in my
    breast,

And I marvel at the havoc mortal passions make
    in life,

Till at last we rest so calmly, dead to every passing
strife ;

And of Denis—ah ! how gladly, I can tell, he was
to lie

In the graveyard on the hillside ; for he had crept
back to die

To the cottage where the roses clamber over
ruined walls,

Where unheeded in the spring-time, all the apple
blossom falls,

And the moonlight soft was flooding as he sought
the casement seat,

All a wreck with roses covered, grass blades tangling round his feet,

And the rosebuds seemed to pity as they touched
his burning head.

Thus 'twas on the casement leaning that they
found him cold and dead ;

But upon his face there lingered such a peaceful,
   loving smile,

That while waiting Death's glad summons, p'raps—
   who knows?—he dreamed awhile,

Dorothy again beside him, and no memory of
   pain ;

Thus Death hastened swiftly, surely, lest life bring
   him back again ;

And I ponder on God's goodness from the hour
   we first draw breath.

Life, O Life ! how could we live thee, if 'twere not
   for thee, O Death ?

# AN AUSTRALIAN FOREST.

I go,—but to return,—

Your dreamy, haunting breeze

Would sing me back again ;

Old friends I might forget,

Old hopes merge in the new,

All, all, but you,—but you.


Your great dark trees would rise

And beckon to my soul ;

I could not wait and know

How cool the autumn mist

Was creeping on the air,

And I—oh ! I not there.

In dreams my eyes would see

The great long golden bars

That lie upon your grass,

When, like a ball, the sun

Rolls down the shining day,

And I,—but I,—away.

I could not live and rest

Far from your wild free trees,

Your branches murmuring,

Your night-bird's distant note ;

To hear each hidden sound

Were happiness profound.

For in the resinous air

That rises mid your trees,

My soul once more could breathe ;

Give me your soughing wind

With perfumed odours blent,

And I,—I am content.

# MIDNIGHT SERVICE.

Silently the midnight air comes stealing o'er the
  land,
Soft breathings of that glorious peace we cannot
  understand,
With infinite calm it hushes, and a touch of awe-
  some fear,
But it seems to us the saddest at the dawning of
  the year.

    For the year lingers,
     A great reality ;
    Ere dawn it will have passed
     To immortality.

Ere dawn I know the poor Old Year, with all its
sobs and sighs,

Shall pass for ever from our life, to a world
beyond the skies ;

And we stand upon the threshold, in wonderment
and fear,

And outside in the darkness we behold the glad
New Year.

But while it lingers,

See ye that ye pray

For God's most high remembrance

Upon this New Year's Day.

As the church clock noiselessly points to that
saddest hour,

We helplessly and dimly feel that the Old Year
and its power

Is waning—waning—waning—as the hands go
  slowly round,—

Ere the New Year's eyes have opened, 'twill have
  fallen to the ground.

  Then, oh ! most humbly
  Bend we the knee ;
  This hour let us dedicate
  Most gratefully to Thee.


It is at such solemn moments that we all devoutly
  pray

That God may cleanse our inmost hearts with
  love on New Year's Day ;

For ere the next New Year is born, ah ! which of
  us can say,

The youngest kneeling in this crowd may they
  have passed away.

G

Ah ! sadly the vanished year

We all review,

And consecrate, with tears,

Some sorrow new.


Oh ! we grieve for a hand we may not press, a face
we loved of yore,

And from our anguished hearts we cry, Would we
had loved it more !

But the church is just a picture of a silent kneeling crowd,

For when our grief is bitterest, it never can be
loud.

On the silent air

Comes a single bell,

'Tis the poor Old Year's

Low, sad death-knell.

Sorrowfully we clutch the moments still within our
keeping,

And all around the silent world seems so
densely sleeping.

Then comes the minister's solemn voice: " Dear
Lord, oh ! let us pray."

And with the sacred hush of death we wait the
New Year's Day.

Hark to the joy bells !

Can the year have fled ?

Ay, a friend has risen,

But a friend is dead.

Yet not quite death—for the Old Year is hovering
near the earth,

What we grieve so much at parting with, we
ushered in with mirth ;

We rang our maddest joy bells then, we sang an
   anthem clear,
And now our brightest cadence is a dirge to
   thee, Old Year.
         Ding, dong, the joy bells
            Fall on the ears
         Of those who have seen
            Full many years.


And falls perchance on a gladsome heart, so full of
   life and joy,
That only the years that come and go can ever
   quite destroy
Her beautiful winsome hope, and faith in all
   things living,
For only those who suffer know that griefs are
   God's own giving.

Ah ! maddening bells,

A New Year is born,

And the Old Year is stealing

Away with the morn.


For only those who try to kiss the power that
holds the rod

Can look behind familiar things, and find the
guise of God,—

Can find a rainbow in their tears, the gleamings
of the sun,

And for the gift of Life cry out, " Thy will, not
mine, be done."

Yea, though the cry

Be wrung with a tear,

We wish a holy Christmas,

And a holier New Year.

# DEATH, THE KING.

In the midst of light and sunshine, and when
    expected least,
Death in his sable mantle stands, a spectre at the
    feast.

We see the altar railings, and we see the happy
    bride,
We see the groups of laughing maids and loving
    friends beside ;
We see the angels standing near to guard them
    with their wing,
We hear the anthem sweet and fresh the village
    children sing,

We see the sunbeams stealing in, we gaze with
bated breath ;

For, standing backward, stern and grim, behold,
the Angel Death.


We see the gay and shining halls, we hear the
music sweet,

Flying along in giddy dance we hear the patt'ring
feet ;

No shadow falls to still the mirth, no quick un-
bidden tear,

The light still shines, the music flows, and all is
happy here ;

But see, just where that curtain falls in festoons
pure and white,

We shudder, for our hearts well know Death
watches here to-night.

The ship flies on, the sailors sing, no cloud is in
the sky,

The heavy washing of the wave melts with the
seagull's cry ;

Each wavelet laughs as though to see how far its
foam could fling,

But on a sullen distant cloud, there rideth Death
the king.


The children laugh upon the grass, and pluck the
blades in glee,

The wind, upon some errand sent, blows past them
fresh and free ;

It taketh life to some poor soul, now fainting for
its breath,

It lightens famine and disease,—it cannot lighten
death.

The happy hunters speed along with hearts as
    light as air,

They fling aside, with lightsome jest, the busy
    phantom care ;

On, on they go, until they race the rushing
    roaring wind,

So full of life and love and light, but Death
    rides on behind.


Then still remember when we join the gay and
    laughing crowd,

The gala dress we wear to-day, to-night may be
    our shroud ;  .

With powerful minds we cannot stay the
    tightened, fleeting breath,

In every throng we know there stands, unasked,
    the Angel Death.

# FRAGMENT.

I TOOK up a flow'ret
All withered and dead,
It was one which had lain
On a fair sweet head.

I gathered the blossom in delicate bloom;

Its fellows have gone with my love to her tomb.

I hold the dry flow'ret, an emblem of grief;

My hopes have all gone with the bloom from its
    leaf.

When life shall have vanished, and sorrow is o'er,

Unite then the blossoms in heaven once more.

∞

# IN THE WEST.

I stood upon the borders of a lake,

    I saw the sun sink crimson in the west;

The stillness and the glamour of the time stole

        o'er me

    Like the vague foreshadowing of eternal rest.


I saw a golden stream of light which shone

    From that wide west, and to my feet it came;

I stept upon that radiant path to journey

    To that bright land of golden-coloured flame.


I saw the islands, with their reeds of crimson;

    I saw each boat, with purple-coloured sail,

Glide on and onward to the emerald ocean,

    While breezes fanned them with a gentle wail.


My steps grew fainter and my pathway dimmer,

    The boats and ocean faded in the sky.

I come back wearily with steps that linger ;

    The night has fallen, and the low winds sigh.

# FLOWERS OF LIFE.

I WAS given some lovely flow'rets,
    Rich crimson and shade of gold ;
The dew of my life in their perfume,
    And heart-throbs in ev'ry fold.
I sheltered the flow'rets and loved them,
    And fancied they always must stay,
And cried out when one drooped and faded
    At the height of my summer's day.

I clung to the rest and caressed them,
    Rebellious in heart when they died ;
And cared not for all that were left me,
    When the brightest drooped at my side.

But passionate tears killed so many —

I dried up my eyes in despair ;

Then I smiled, and I saw as I did so,

How lovely the blossoms still there.


Though some of the tenderest faded,

And some of the strongest fell ;

I now let them go with submission,

My heart had ceased to rebel

And now my bright bunch of sweet blossoms

Have fallen away to so few,

That my innermost heart can hold them,

With the flowers that perished too.

# A REMEMBRANCE.

A SINGLE long-lost chord, the echo of an old refrain,

Can bring back buried memories and waken grief
    again ;

When, laughing, in the midst we stand of some
    gay, thoughtless throng,

A sweet old air will startle us, and tenderly we
    long

To live again, for one short hour, the dreams of
    long ago,

To fling away despairingly the crushing load of
    woe.

Perhaps some evening in the gloam will come
    before our eyes,

The loaded air, with many flowers, beneath the
　　sunny skies ;

Some girlish form we loved too well that tender
　　air had sung,

And mem'ry travels back, and brings the days
　　when we were young.

But music only thus can bring the weary depths
　　that lie

Beneath the gaily smiling lips, the bright and
　　sparkling eye,

Beneath the laughter low and sweet, the bright
　　and careless word,

For music strikes the hidden chord, and sorrow's
　　depths are stirred.

# THE TIDE OF LIFE.

## AN ALLEGORY.

I saw a lovely Leaflet fall into a streamlet wide,

It stayed an instant where it fell, then floated from
  the side ;

At first it glided softly on beneath the azure sky,

Then brushed and almost sank against a bough
  that floated by ;

It rose again, but in the bough there must have
  been a thorn,

For all the green and lovely edge was sadly spoiled
  and torn ;

The stream yet sang—the sky as blue—and still it
  floated on,

The water hid each jagged edge, but there was

something gone ;

The freshness and the loveliness that marked it as

it fell

Had passed away invisibly, until one scarce could

tell

That in its tender gracefulness there ever could

have been

Upon that freshly verdant leaf a sweeter, purer

green.


And now it passed upon its way, until a sudden

break

Revealed, embowered with sedge's wave, a restful,

sleeping lake,

And here the waters scarcely stirred to ripple on

each bank—

No sound except the lily-bells, that slowly rose and
    sank ;

But near it ran a rapid stream, where sun and
    shadow lay,

They chased each other from their path throughout
    the livelong day ;

Here tall rocks rose, and scarce a flower could grow
    beneath their shade—

In wonder at the stream and lake the little Leaflet
    stayed ;

It paused an instant then, to choose which onward
    course to take,

The rapid roaring river, or the flower-decked,
    peaceful lake.


A Straw came floating carelessly from where the
    Leaflet came,

It started from the old oak tree, its course had
  been the same ;
It stayed a little, gained the lake, then touched the
  Leaflet's side,
Though light its touch, it changed its course into
  the torrent wide ;
And now 'twas hurried rapidly—no time to dream
  or stay ;
The waters, in their urgent haste, had swept it on
  its way.


Now tossed upon the ocean's wave a withered
  Leaflet dreams
Of distant shores, bedecked with flowers, beside
  the murm'ring streams ;
By vessels passing on their way the Leaflet is not
  seen ;

But lone seagulls the song may sing of hopes that
might have been.

'Twas even so a young life passed before my tear-
dimmed eyes ;
A Leaflet on Life's rapid course it sank, no more
to rise.
I could not stay it, though I knew how dark the
water's roar ;
With folded hands I trusted it to God for evermore.

# A FOREST SHRINE.

FOREST free ! I bring my sadness for the last time
to your heart ;

'Tis that last sad, solemn moment when I come
and say, " We part " ;

I will gaze upon your branches, I will hear each
rustling sound,

Even to the leaves that circle as they flutter to the
ground ;

Crisp the grey-green leaves beneath me, blue the
sky that peeps between,

As a turquoise to the emerald of your branches
glossy green.

Now these things are near me, with me ; when the
sun shall set again,

Nothing but my prayers can reach them, only
   memory will remain ;

But, beholding, I would print them on my sight in
   one long gaze,

That my heart-thoughts may recall them as they
   are, in coming days—

Days that hold of joy or sadness what I, mortal,
   cannot see,

Only knowing that all your beauty will remain, but
   not for me.

Forest ! standing as I stand now, something from
   your heart meets mine,

Something in your solemn grandeur—for your lofty
   trees combine

To annul the self within me that, being base, would
   cling to earth,

From your inspiration holy comes my better spirit's
   birth ;

For the thoughts that have no naming rise like
    anthems on the breeze,

And in time association blends them with your
    stormy trees.

Years have passed since men at parting consecrated
    at some shrine

All life's holies; thus, O Forest! I will consecrate
    at thine

What is best and truest in me, what expands when
    some deep joy

Vibrates all my soul within me, vibrates without
    self alloy.

Forest mighty! Father Forest! as I gaze on some
    worn tree,

Lo, a benediction holy from your wind-song comes
    to me;

So I dedicate my future to the influence—that I
    know—

That I fear and dread will weaken, in life's steady
    downward flow,

In the petty needs of living, in the trifles that
    assume

All importance in the weaving of our hour-by-hour
    life-loom.

Forest ! could your greatness linger in my heart, as
    on this day,

I might combat those great problems that retard
    our upward way,

For my soul when here flies outward, as some bird
    from broken bars,

And I would that I could leave it, here amid the
    trees and stars ;

Better that than drag its plumage through the fret
    of life below ;

Safe within your great heart's keeping, I should find
    it white as snow ;

For I feel that though my eyesight, chained with
    limits, ne'er shall see

On this earth the actual beauty of each wind-blown
    flower and tree,

Yet when death shall break the binding from my
    mortal, sightless eyes,

In the splendour of your greatness will my soul's
    first anthem rise.

# IN MEMORIAM.

## (An Australian Poet.)

We call him dead. Why dead? Such words have
    grown
To empty sounds from which the soul has flown.
Not death, but life, the dawn where he can see
God's wondrous reason for mortality.
The songs he sung were all of that last birth,
As though he had outgrown the things of Earth,
As though his soul its limits had outrun,
And burst with thoughts the veil that hid the sun
"Tween beauty here and perfectness beyond
He saw and felt the grand unbroken bond—

The one pure thing, the food of souls on earth,

The anthem, sung to life, to make it worth

The while to live, to grieve, rejoice, and then

To pass, as clouds, from out the world of men.

All things he wrote he felt, and suffered first ;

His faith to him was not some wild outburst

Of passion's play, but truth, absorbing, deep,—

Unbroken life,—Death's change a moment's sleep.

Then do not call him dead, because this stage

Of his immortal life has turned a page ;

Instead rejoice that at one joyous bound

Perfected life and love his soul has found.

# IN MEMORIAM.

Farewell ! The mem'ry of thy sweet-lined face

Shall live among us in thy vacant place ;

Thy life, devoted to unselfish cares,

Formed bright processions of unspoken prayers,

And lived and blossomed in thy gentle breast,

The unseen pathway to eternal rest.

Our tears are falling for ourselves, not thee,

Clad in thy Father's matchless sanctity,

The broken partings of thy life fulfilled,

Thy hopes and sorrows and thy yearnings stilled ;

But our regrets, dear, when we miss thy face,

Thy form and smile, from thine accustomed place,

Are things not measured by a day or year,

A lifelong missing is thy tribute, dear.

Sweetly and humbly did thy virtues grow,

As violets earthward, with their petals low ;

The self-abasing which would not repine—

A life so lovely must be half divine.


Oh ! lives, still struggling for some earthly prize,

Look back one moment with your saddened eyes ;

Her life, unlaurelled save in hearts of love,

Has won the kingdom of the blest above,

And was, we feel it, as we stand alone,

Still something better to have lived and known.

# IN MEMORIAM.

Oh ! touch the lute gently that echoes his
    name ;
It ceased as it breathed on the mirror of fame,
One moment reflected, —the next, and we know
That the hopes of the poet have vanished like
    snow,—
As melting it lingers, yet scarce on the earth,
Then vanishes slowly, a death in a birth.
Oh ! death with thy shadow, what hopes hast thou
    slain,
As judged by the fragments of gems that
    remain !

Then, night-winds, sweep softly, and spring breezes
    blow,
A requiem to chant to the young hopes laid low ;
One sigh for his fate and for fond hearts bereft,
Then joyously turn we to thoughts he has left.

# A REPENTANCE.

I STOOD and listened in the shadow, where I knew

    his feet must pass,

I could tell them in a thousand, though they

    echoed on the grass.

I had bit my lips so firmly, lest they utter trem-

    bling sound ;

And my hands were clasped so tightly, that my

    heart, in honour bound,

Would not tell him of its throbbing, though I

    heard each steady beat ;

By-and-by with awful rhythm it would measure to

    his feet.

Not a moment then passed by me, only hours with
    leaden stride, -

I could see the daisies flowering and the painted
    pea outside ;

I could hear some dead leaves falling from the
    far-off old oak tree ;

I could hear the sparrows calling, blithely twit-
    tering, happy, free ;

I could hear a brown bee droning, as he went from
    flower to flower ;

All these sounds went on and passed me, could
    not wake me with their power,

And I saw my hands were twisted, white and rigid
    without pain ;

Did I live, or had my spirit once more taken flight
    again ?

Were these sights and sounds familiar, near me,
    by me, or away

In some other strange existence, an eternal summer's day ?

I could see the sunlight falling, as its wont was
near the door,

Yet I watched it wondering, curious, as a thing
not seen before,

And beyond all sound and senses, all in all one
fierce long wait

For a step that must come surely, entering at the
iron gate.

Just then sorrows,—past and future,—all were
merged into that sense

Of such waiting, watching, longing, blotting out
all self-pretence.

Was it hours since first I stood there, or had years
gone slowly by ?

All that time I shall remember clearly only when
I die.

In the distance, hark ! a footfall, throbbed my heart
    to every sound,

As a walker still in dreamland, as a prisoner I was
    bound ;

Not for words or uttered welcome would my tight-
    ened tongue obey,

Other lips I knew would greet him, mine alone
    have nought to say ;

Yes, his footsteps still were coming, and I heard
    their every sound,

Like a mighty weight of iron, crushing, crushing
    on the ground.

With a firm and steady rhythm, each one sounding
    out apart,

As in falling, fell they closer, till they stepped upon
    my heart.

Years ago a wrong was uttered, years ago, and
    now to-day,

Only in my heart was beating all my tensioned
   lips would say.

Deep repentance, expiation, humble vears for one
   hour's sin ;

For this meeting I had hungered, loved him
   truly,—should love win ?

Now the steps were so close to me, just another
   turn, and then

He would see me,—if he doubt me, proudly he
   would turn again.

And the brown bee still was working, flitting on
   from flower to flower ;

I could see these things and know them in this
   last, last meeting hour.

Ceased the footsteps, and I knew it, though my
   trembling lips were dumb,

And my eyes cast down were stiffened, as he said
   but one word—" Come."

# THE FIRST EASTER DAWN.

THE mystic darkness of the midnight lonely
  Lies heavily around,
And purple shadows, in their deepness only,
  Brood o'er the silent ground.

A pause in living and in animation,
  When sound and silence meet :
A pause, when heart-throbs of the great creation
  Faintly and slowly beat.

The long, deep rolling of the ceaseless ocean
  Falls not with breaking sound ;
The dim suggestion of its dreary motion
  Makes silence more profound.

The streets are silent ; on the haunts of sorrow
    Kind night has laid her hand,
And no foretelling of the grief to-morrow
    Can make the hour less grand.

Forth, through the cumb'ring of the shadows
      blinding,
    A faint, long streak of light
Tells of the secret that the hours are finding
    Behind the cloak of night.

Lo ! the streak broadens, and a dim reflection
    Glimmers on oceans wide,
And on two angels who, with sweet protection,
    Are watching side by side.

Whitely before them gleams the coming morning,
    Lighting the cold, dark sky ;
Heralding glories of the sun's adorning,
    As hand in hand they fly.

Pause they a moment, for they bring the token,
    Carried from out the gloom ;
The blest assurance that our life unbroken
    Arises from the tomb.


Faint streaks of crimson with the white are
      mingling—
    Fair raiment for the morn ;
With hope and glory all the earth is tingling
    Upon this Easter dawn.


Leave it in freshness, as a wild rose blooming—
    Oh ! leave the coming day—
The depth of darkness in its light entombing,
    Beneath the angels' way.

# AUSTRALIAN RECOLLECTIONS.

' Tis oh ! for the sight of a forest wild,

    Where the lengthening sunbeams lay

Like golden strips on the verdant grass

    At the close of the summer's day !

The tall grey limbs enwrapped with green,

    The ultramarine of the sky,

The trees of wattle with golden flecks

    We brushed, as we hastened by—

That filled the air with their perfume sweet,

    That laughed in their yellowy blaze,

For a canter 'neath the fragrant trees,

    For a dream of the sweet old days.

The tender low of a drowsy herd
    As they wend to the water's brink,
And flowers cast in by a laughing child
    Float by as they slowly drink.

The horses wild, with high, arched neck
    And a frightened, graceful look,
As we passed would turn, and bound away
    To the shade of some leafy nook ;

Then curious stand when far away,
    And whinny aloud —as, half scared,
They gather from out the valleys near
    The rest of the startled herd.

The jackass laughs above in the trees,
    And the curlew wails from afar,
The sun sinks down behind the blue hill
    As rises the evening star.

The shadows have gone, the night has come,

    And soon will the shimmering moon

Begin to glimmer her snowy white

    On the breast of the still lagoon.


The day is past in the forest deep,

    Where the slanting sunbeams lay,

The trees will sleep in the moon's soft light—

    Thus closes Australia's day.


So though I waken in other lands,

    My heart thoughts ever must stray

Where deepening shadows fall, I know,

    In the forests at close of the day.

# SUMMER.

GLORIOUS Child of the Sun !

   Born with his gold on thy face ;

Singing the song of the ripening grain,

Opening flowers, that for months have lain

   Wrapped in the earth's embrace ;

Warming each bud with thy quickening breath,

Triumphant and scorning the spirit of Death.

Glorious Child of the Sun !

   Born with his crown on thy hair ;

Girdled with flowers that bloomed for thy sake

Trailing thy garments by river and lake,

   Waking the melodies there ;

Death springs to life where thy kisses have lain,

Life is thine anthem and Love its refrain.

# AN AUSTRALIAN SUNSET.

WITHOUT, the birds are singing sweetest anthems
in the trees,

And the sound is softly floated and borne upon
the breeze ;

The sun has shed his radiance, and is passing from
our sight,

Yet casts one flush of tenderness ere leaving us to-
night.

The glory of that spell-bound hour, that silent, last
farewell,

Ah ! poetry can never paint ; ah ! weak heart
ne'er can tell ;

•

For lo ! what hand has been at work  upon that
   tintless sky ?

Rich billowy clouds of golden hue  upon its bosom
   lie ;

An  instant  since  one  great  expanse  of  soft  unbroken blue,

And  now  a  bold  artistic  hand  has  painted  every
   hue,

From a crimson   such a crimson !   seen  ne'er but
   in the sky ;

Perhaps  it  is  the  shadow  cast  of  robes  to  wear on
   high,

Perhaps  it  is  the  weary  sun,  ere  leaving  for
   awhile,

Casts  back  a  lingering  look  at  earth,  a  farewell
   rosy smile :

And  then  a  thousand  mingled  tints  that  sweep
   across the gold,

A thousand hues that come to light as rainbow
    gleams unfold.
We hold our breath, we gaze entranced; but even
    as we gaze,
Between us and the sun's last glance there falls the
    summer haze ;
And now the gold has melted, and amidst the
    crimson's hue
The sky with dreamy sadness is unfolding in its
    blue.
  Tisthus one instant, perfect, grand, ere passing
    from our sight,—
The spell is gone : we turn, and lo ! we meet the
    shadowy night ;
An instant more the stars are out, the sunset tale
    is told,
A steadfast grey of purest shade has chased the
    living gold ;

God's messenger, it seemed to me, had passéd from
   our sight
And taken records, writ in gold, of earthly things
   to-night.

# THE POETRY OF LIFE.

I HAVE not from past traditions truest inspiration

    found,

Rather solved those silent sorrows that are every-

    where around.

Splendid myths for poets' weaving lie, I know, in

    old-world lore,

Tales of flowers, and gods, and syrens, visions that

    exist no more.

But, I think, life's patient heart-cry, with its tragic

    undertone,

Is a stronger chord to waken than perfections that

    have flown ;

For I know sad hearts are beating, parted wide by

    sea and land,

And these songs—if you will sing them—they will

    hear and understand ;

For the key of life is sadness, joy the sunshine

    through the leaves ;

Touch this note and sing it truly,—you will reach

    some heart that grieves.

Of all fields where fancies wander for a theme to

    weave in song,

Human passions are the truest, none reverberate

    so long.

Beauteous songs and dreamy fancies, that like

    swallows upward soar

Out of sound of human heart-cries to that mystic

    world of lore ;

Sunny hours, in life's first morning, did I owe to

    that grand flight,

Till I found that golden sunrise slowly deepened

> into night ;

Then I turned and learnt the music that is set to

> life around,

And my half-fledged dreams and fancies found a

> foothold on the ground.

So my songs are as I found them, writ in life, and

> their refrain,

When the songs shall long have left me, some sore

> heart will sing again.

# ALWAYS.

THERE are always storms of sorrow rising
    Impalpable as air ;
We cannot hear the moans or feel the writhings
    Of their mute despair.


There are always thousands seeking dumbly
    A foothold for the soul ;
In one guise or another, calling always,
    " Master, make me whole ! "

# A DREAM.

An army of angels I saw at a gate :

The one who came first was the angel of fate ;

And the angel who shone in radiance above,

I knew by his glory was angel of love.

An angel was there with a glittering crown,

Bright, bright were the rays that fell flickering
   down ;

And fair was his face with the roundness of
   youth,—

That angel, I felt, was the angel of truth.

The angel who knelt with a low-bended head,

As mortals will weep for their much-beloved dead,

Was angel of mercy, compassion, and rest,

And that was the angel I knew I loved best.

# AN IDEAL.

A LAND of poppies, and of cornfields yellow,
  A land of perfectness and rest and flowers,
A day of idleness from toil and stirring,
  A something to remember in the weary hours.
The cattle, winding with their steady footsteps,
  Go one by one across the waving plain,
The children laughing as they pick the flowerets,
  The roses clambering in the dewy lane.

# A VISION OF LIFE.

Hush ! the Christmas winds are sighing,

And the Christmas sunlight dying

  Out upon the silent sod,

And of every gift He sends us,

And of every gem He lends us,

  This alone returns to God.

So, before the land shall darken,

I would have the sunlight hearken,

  On this fading Christmas-tide,

To the tale of just one mortal,

So that at the heavenly portal

  They may enter side by side.

See a girl in youth's fresh glory,

All impatient for life's story ;

   See a Vision close at hand,

That shall lure her in the dawning

Of her young heart's glorious morning,

   Out into the shaded land.


Ah ! it laughs and bends to greet her,

Though the white hands never meet her,

   Still they keep a happy wave ;

And the graceful steps are dancing,

But receding, not advancing,

   With a young life for its slave.


See the fields with lilies blowing,

See the crimson poppies growing

   Out among the bending grass ;

For the fairest flowers seem brighter,

And the heavy shadows lighter,

    As the Vision's footsteps pass.


Now it flits without a warning,

In the glow of life's glad dawning,

    'Neath a grand cathedral door ;

And the organ's notes are pealing,

And the sun, through windows stealing,

    Falls in patches on the floor.


All around the trace of ages—

Passed now unto memory's pages-—

    Live in majesty of awe ;

And the stately walls age-darkened,

And the bygone souls that hearkened,

    In the grey years gone before.

Now the organ ceases pealing,

As before the altar kneeling,

    With the Vision at her side,

See the girl it lured so brightly,

With its laughter falling lightly,

    Now a dreaming, trustful bride.


See, the Vision o'er her bending,

Lest she see Life's shades descending,

    Sees, and from the mirage turns,—

Turns away in quick derision

From the fair evading Vision,

    And life's saddest story learns.


So it points with sweet beguiling,

And its red lips ever smiling,

    To a path it wreaths with flowers ;

Through the cornfields waving golden,

Still it whispers legends olden,

    To beguile the passing hours.


Cries the Vision, " Roses clamber,

Scented white and paling amber,

    And the rich pomegranates bloom ;"

But spoke not of yews surrounding,

And the cypress trees abounding,—

    Flowers they plant upon a tomb.


Then it waves with sweet deluding,

'Mid the scent from flowers exuding,

    Fruits from every distant land ;

As the girl exulting grasps them,

They, the instant that she clasps them,

    Turn to ashes in her hand.

But, when she in wonder grieving
Cries, "The Vision is deceiving,"
        Flash before her dazzled gaze
Crowns of gems in beauty gleaming
And around, in radiance streaming,
        Falls a phosphorescent haze.


And she drops the ruins unheeding,
While her eager heart is feeding
        On the gems before her eyes ;
But when she has grasped their shining
As an icy snake entwining,
        Half their glowing lustre dies.


Then when she in sorrow calling,
Hears the Vision's music falling
        Soothingly upon her heart ;

But the lutes when she would sound them,

All the harmony around them

    Into strangest discords start ;


And it does not soothe, but saddens,

For life's beauty never gladdens,

    Falling on an empty soul.

One by one life's joys departed,

They have left her weary hearted :

    Learning grief is pleasure's toll.


And the girl who in life's morning,

With her fresh youth's fair adorning,

    Passed alone into the fight,

She remembers vaguely dreaming,

As a thing that once had seeming,

    Veiled now in the gloom of night.

Still the Vision laughs glad laughter,

Fleeing self, she follows after,

    Through a pleasant mossy lane,

Where the sunset rays are gleaming

On the scented flow'rets, streaming

    From the recent gentle rain.


And she, tired, in sadness follows

O'er the undulating hollows,

    As the leaves are turning brown ;

Lo ! before her, without warning,

Falls a chasm, widely yawning,

    Darkling thousand fathoms down.


And the Vision points down singing,

And the hanging rocks are ringing

    With the echo of each tone.

" See ! " it cries, " the flowers are blooming,

Down there in their mossy tombing ; "

    But the answer is a groan.


See a woman mute with sorrow,

One who dreads the dawning morrow,

    Turning from the Vision's side ;

But its tone for ever haunts her,

As she flies, it idly taunts her

    With the follies she would hide.


Without guidance she is flying,

And she sees the sunlight dying,

    Out into the tinted west.

And her heart for peace is thirsting,

With life's sins too nearly bursting,

    Till she sinks her down to rest.

Suddenly before her bending,

'Mid the shades of night descending,

   Stands a Vision clad in grey ;

And it smiles in tender sadness,

Underlying gentle gladness,

   As the April sunlight's ray.


So it essays its first healing,

As the Christmas bells come stealing

   Soothingly along the lea ;

And it told the sweet old story

Of that lowly birth and glory,

   And the things that are to be.


And the woman listened humbling,

Heart and soul, whilst from her crumbling

   All the old life slowly fell.

And she heard the people talking

Humbly, yet so happ'ly walking,

    To the church and ringing bell.


As each happy peal decreases,

And the rolling echo ceases,

    Comes an organ's cadence low.

Cries the woman, " May I follow

To the church in yonder hollow,—

    I, sin-spattered, may I go ? "


Then she followed, kneeling lowly,

Listening to the lesson holy,

    Words she scarcely seemed to know.

Mutely praying, she felt her weakness,

Hearing of that life of meekness

    Spent in sorrow here below.

L

And she prayed, **not** words unmeaning,

Idle eyes and light thoughts screening,

But a self-abasing cry.

Written in immortal pages,

Carried to the Rock of Ages,

With a humble sinner's sigh.


This was all ; no wine was broken,

Neither gold nor silver token,

Yet a weary woman came

From the silent church, sin-pardoned—

Prayer softens hearts, though hardened

With a life of grief and shame.


Now the Christmas winds are sighing,

And the happy sunlight dying

Out upon the silent sod ;

But of every gift He sends us,

And of every gem He lends us,

  This alone returns to God.


So I pray it take this story,

That it enter in the glory

  Of a shining sunbeam's ray.

For I know true joy's best feeling

Lies in grief around us healing,

  And in purer passion's sway.


And the sorrows born in sadness,

Reap a harvest of such gladness,

  That they must by God be sent.

Very soon the land will darken,

But perhaps some soul may hearken

  Ere the Christmas-tide be spent.

# A REMINISCENCE.

To-night I heard the very song

That you and I, in days long gone

    Would softly sing together.

Ah ! dear, your image comes before ;

I know the very dress you wore,

    And in your hair some heather.


I left the singer and the room ;

I paced beside your silent tomb

    Until the early dawn ;

For we are parted evermore,

And you have reached the other shore,

    Whilst I am here forlorn.

Oh! that another dared to sing

Words you loved; ah, me! they bring

   The thoughts of other years,

When our voices happily blended

As through fragrant lanes we wended,—

   And I am mute with tears.


Farewell! how prized your mem'ry still,

When e'en a careless song can will

   The long-forbidden tears,

And my heart is torn with anguish!

Ah! my love, for you I languish

   After all these weary years.


Oh! if I could only press

Your little hand in tenderness,

   Its touch my soul would tell.

Can I forget thee ? thou wert mine !

As well the stars could cease to shine,—

Beloved, fare thee well.

# AN AUSTRALIAN EVENING HYMN.

THE day is done.

    Into the forest glades the night has passed,

        Out in the stretching fields the evening

        nun,

    Grey in her twilight robes, follows her fast ;

        Murmurs that rose all day, sounds of the

        Sun,

        Sink with the windy breeze,—the day is

        done.

Toil stands asleep.

    Dropped from his nerveless hand the sickle

        lies ;

The windlass rope sways out, the toilers

creep

Home by the well-worn paths; the last light

dies;

Fires from the opened doors gleam one by

one,

Speaking of love within.   The day is done.


The darkened land

Deep in cool slumber rests, while on the hills,

Lifting the heavy clouds, the Moon's white

hand

Slowly the wide, dark world with wonder fills;

Light of a paler day, wraith of the Sun,

Queen of the purple night when day is

done.

# AUSTRALIA EXULTANS.

## SONG OF THE DAWN.

IN the wonderful light of a golden dawn,

From the wet, salt surges, a child was born ;

And it laughed to its sire – the immortal Sun—

Time trembled the glass, that the sands might

    run :

And it lulled to their sound as the streams sang

    by,

Its robe was the blue of the infinite sky ;

And sleeping or laughing, the hands that were

    curled

As sea-shells, held prisoned a hope for the world.

## SONG OF THE FOREST.

HEAR ye not the forest branches rustling in the

happy breeze ?

Hear ye not the forest voices speaking softly from

the trees ?

Telling of those years of silence buried in the vast

unknown,

When they caught and kept the freedom that has

swelled into their tone,

When they saw the sun in grandeur unregarded

roll to rest,

Saw him shed the selfsame glory that he now

sheds in the west,

Saw how all the wild flowers blossomed, gems of

light on hill and vale ;

And in time these things were woven by the wind

into their tale.

## Song of the Stars.

Long have the crystal stars unbroken vigil kept

Through dim, forgotten years, when white waves
    roaring swept

The lonely, lovely shores, to die upon their breast.

Stars, tell your changing tale; you saw the long,
    long rest

Of those uncounted years break into life; you
    saw

The ocean's tossing waste grow white with sails,—
    its roar

No more made plaintive sound to nature's ear
    alone,

But happy children laughed upon its shores; their
    tone

New lonely echoes woke, and shouts of ringing
    glee

The tireless anthems swelled of surging wind and
  sea.

Your shining, steadfast eyes have seen the new
  life flow,

At first in trembling streams, then quickly braver
  grow,

Until the wide, wild waves of its existence swept

O'er plains and shaded vales where happy nature
  slept.

----

## SONG OF THE CENTURY.

OH ! beautiful, sinless child of the world,
    Born in its grey old age ;
To-day the first fold in your flag is unfurled,
    To-day an unstainèd page

Is turned in the book of your virginal past,

 Whiter than wind-fluttered snow ;

Whiter than blossoms e'er wild winds have cast

 Their leaves on the earth below.

Oh ! love and protect her, ye sons of the land,

 Keep in its unsullied grace

This crystalline record she bears in her hand,

 The sunshine of God in her face.

---

## SONG OF PRAISE.

GLORY to Thee, O God !   The restless seas

Thunder the great refrain ; the forest trees

Murmur the same low chant ; the streamlet tells

The reeds upon its banks ; the bird-note swells

The same triumphant strain.   Lord, let us raise

Our voice to loftier tones to sing Thy praise.

Glory to Thee, O God! This sun-lit land,

Sweet with scented flowers fresh from Thy hand,

Leads us to nobler ways. Lord, shall not we

Ever by its white light aspire to Thee?

Glory to Thee, O God! the song outpour,

Glory and praise be Thine—Thine evermore.

# A CHRISTMAS WISH.

A SUNBEAM taken from the plenty here,

To melt thy snowflakes, I would send thee,

    dear,—

The blue that slumbers in Australia's skies

Seems but reflected from thy radiant eyes.

The flowers that blossom in the forest shade,

A pathway only for thy feet seem made ;

So, flowers and sunbeams with the blue entwine,

A message taken from my heart to thine.

# OUT OF THE PAST.

To-DAY in one short instant came the dream I
   ne'er forget,
'Twas wafted on my senses by the breath of
   mignonette ;
I was but musing idly, as I watched a river's flow,
My thoughts had wandered widely from the haunts
   of long ago.
But from memory's borderland that mignonette
   had crept,
And o'er my soul in agony a tide of feelings swept :
And the meadow and the trees, the evening's
   dreamy light

Were darkened in an instant, and were blotted

from my sight,

By visions of what might have been by desolate

despair ;

The lost ones from the past arise, and stay to

haunt me there ;

For they clasp me with their hands, and they woo

me with their tones,

But I shudder from their touch, and I answer

them with groans.

Ah ! they have reached a fairer land, whilst I am

toiling here,

And on the grave-yard of the past I drop a silent

tear ;

For I see them slowly melting and fading in the

air,

I feel no more the tangling of the meshes of their

hair ;

M

I stagger back again to life, the mignonette is
   gone,
With tearless eyes resume my cross, and slowly
   struggle on.

# GONE.

Now hushed is the lyre and mute is the lay,

The dear ones who loved them have vanished

    away ;

No more shall their tones on my solitude break,

No more shall their songs the dread silence awake.


For I ne'er may now waken the sounds that I love,

Lest the strains of my music should reach them

    above.


The fire-light that flickers attunes to my heart

As it fitfully rises and gleams with a start ;

Like the loved and the lost, and joys that have
flown,

They have left an old man to dream here alone.

Yet I linger ere touching the chords that I love,

Lest the sound of an echo should reach them
above.


The flowers which we gathered, the books which
we read,

Are numbered by me with the past and the dead.

The grief which I shroud lest the world should
descry,

And mock at the anguish the callous deny.

From the songs they loved best I refrain for their
sake,

Lest the sound of my music should bid them
awake.

To awaken and hear me with anguish and fears;

To drop on my lone lot their sweet angel tears,

Ah! no, they now rest from the whirlwinds of

strife,

And not for vain sorrow shall come back to life.

Then oh! rest, ye adored ones, in heaven above,

Till together we waken the strains that I love.

# DEATH.

A SHUDDERING, long-drawn sigh,

A heavy, tightened breath,

An instant of bewilderment,

And mortals call it " Death."

It is the triumphant freeing of a spirit on its way,

To where joy fadeth not, and where sorrow cannot

stay ;

To put on life immortal, as a newer, holier birth,

And to hear in full in heaven the fragments learned

on earth ;

To exchange for the light of God an uncertain,

fitful breath,

To dwell in the soul of righteousness,—and men

have called it Death.

# WAITING.

LOOKING with vague-shadowed eyes,

Filled with curious half-surprise,

Out toward  hat wide, wide sea,

Between her and eternity.

What lies there ?   She dreams and dreams ;

Golden isles and shining streams ?

Placid lakes or sunset glows ?

To go or stay she scarcely knows.

Yet how strange—like hidden bells —

Something sweet, mysterious tells

Words of that old tale, that yet

Her life shall to music set.

Her soul has held the clue so long

To that divine melodious song,

That all the chords are strung, and she

In love shall find life's symphony.

# HER BIRTHDAY.

I LOOKED outside at dawn, that grey, cool hour,
  When life and noise are still ;
I saw its first faint glimmer gaining power
  ·Behind the eastern hill.


I watched the shadows break, until the sky
  Was one wide arch of light ;
And breezes, floating round me, seemed to sigh
  A requiem to the night.


But though I prayed it, still the sunshine tarried
  On this day of all days,

When I had hoped it might have safely carried

My heart's-love on its rays.


But, even as I thought it, one long ray

Of gold shot from the night,

And all the world, but now so dim and grey,

Was turned to golden light.


I said, " 'Tis well that this thy birthday, dear,

Should hold an omen bright;

And show, though shadows darken, somewhere

near

There lies the golden light.


" 'Thus, dearest, may it shine whene'er the clouds

Are darkest in thy sky;

That sorrow may not hide the joy it shrouds

To give thee by-and-by.

" And lighten, dear, thy birthday here on earth,

    Till, life's short journey done,

Immortal sunshine cheers another birth,

    A holier life begun."

# THE NIGHT HAS FALLEN.

THE night has fallen like a spell of peace upon the
earth,

The shadows crouch like mantles round the trees
that gave them birth,

The lilac blooms are dulled to white, the jasmine
stars shine out,

The hour is one sweet melody, yet memories are
about.

How sad a perfume or a flower in after years may
be,

When recollection is but grief, and joy a memory!

With brilliant eyes the young may stand and drink
in some new scene;

To older eyes, alas ! alas ! a shadow falls between.

On yonder belt of meadow-land and mountains
  mossed with green

Dear ones stood round,—not thus alone I first
  beheld that scene.

For shadows of the past are round each grassy hill
  and dale ;

What spot has not some record kept of tears without avail ?

# HOW STILL THE HOUSE IS!

How still the house is now, how strangely still !
    The dark'ning blinds are drawn against the
        pane ;
Upon the flowers that twine around the sill
    The droning bees make murmurs, as of rain.


But yesterday the wheel's melodious whir
    Made music in the low, old-fashioned room ;
Sounds came and went instinct with cheerful stir ;
    Why wrapped to-day in still and soundless
        gloom ?

To-day the blinds are closed, for Death has
  brought
  Into the house his agonized repose ;
But on the floors lie sunbeams which have fought
  Their way into this house of heavy woes.


Be patient then, the blinds will raise again,
  The bees will startle from the opened sill ;
To-morrow come, this gloom will not remain,—
  You will not find the house again so still.


Oh ! silence thou who speakest to me there ;
  How dost thou know, though rooms are opened
    wide
And gladsome sounds float out upon the air,
  Where floated out the soul of her who died—

But that some one has closed for aye the sill,

    Has shut the sunshine out from crick and door ;

That to some heart 'twill always be as still,

    As silent, hushed and still, for evermore?

# A CHRISTMAS SONG.

A song, a song, a Christmas song ;
    A song of the summer's golden sloth,
    A sun that lingers as though he were loth
To quit his kingdom, the sky, for long,
        And leave the moon triumphant.

Oh ! sweet human love, in sunshine or snow
Breathe into life's marble the same fervid glow.

A song, a song, a Christmas song,
    Sung in the sweet Australian clime ;
    The first, first note of that Christmas chime
Was struck in the year agone so long
        On the shores of Galilee.

And the strange, rare sound in the woods was
   heard,
And the carol was sung by a forest bird.

A song, a **song,** a Christmas song ;
   A song to sing in a white, white land,
   **Where the** burning torch and the lurid **brand**
**Of sorrow** and crime and sickening wrong
      Lie still-**born in** the dawning.

**From** the restlessness **of our** sins to-day
We shall pluck the mist of our doubts away.

A song, a song, a **Christmas song,**
   **To sing** in a land where **the** sunbeams bide,
   Where over the hills **on the distant side**
May stand, and we know not, the heavenly throng,
      Sweet orisons intoning.

We offer the soul of a Christmas prayer
To God and His angels standing there.

# A DAY'S FLIGHT.

MORNING bursting,

Day-flowers thirsting

    For the yellow, happy sun,

Blue-bells ringing,

Dewdrops swinging,

    Vanish ere the day is done.


Raindrops quiver,

Gleam, and shiver

    On the web the spider weaves ;

Night and morning,

Day and dawning,

    One day less for sorrow leaves.

179

Sunset dying,

Birds are flying

    In the dim reflected light,

From the fountains

To the mountains—

    To their rest upon the height.


Young things thinking,

Young hearts drinking,

    While the earth to them is young

Shadows creeping,

Mourners weeping,

    And the little song is sung.

# A FORESHADOWING.

WHERE the tallest grasses grow, and shadows

flicker to and fro,

There would I lie ;

And those kneel beside who love me, planting

immortelles above me,—

Not flowers that die.


Lay me where the happy sun shines brightly till

his work is done,

Not in deep shade ;

But an undulating spot, some mossy, green, and

peaceful grot,

Or open glade.

Do not lay me all alone, afar from loving friends
and home,

      Lonely and sad ;

But where music of the bells the sabbath church-
time sweetly tells,—

      Then am I glad.


Keep me in your hearts, I pray ; 'tis all I ask, but
that I may

      At pleasure roam

In the dim and silent halls, amid the ivy-covered
walls

      Of my loved home.

# A PASSING BELL.

HARK ! the bell tolling, for some one is dead ;

Then cease the gay laughter and hush the loud

    tread.

That some one's life-journey is ended, we know ;

Their summer is over, their winter and snow ;

Their hopes and despairings, their sorrows and

    fears,

And mourners are weeping sad, sorrowful tears.

A funeral is passing, bare the bowed head,

The bell keeps repeating that " some one is dead."

But I think, when I hear a bell's measured toll,

That we should rejoice with the bondage-freed

    soul.


Freed !    Past the blue mountains and ocean's

    white foam,

Enwrapped in the peace of a heavenly home.

# A FAIRY WISH.

I HOLD a wish, dear, that a bright-eyed fairy
    Once told me I might spend
On any project, brilliant, bright, and airy,
    Or give it to a friend.

But years of gladness, each with joyous seasons,
    Across my path have flown,
And still for many valid human reasons
    My wish remains my own.

But now I give it with life's other treasures
    To smile upon your way :
" That joy may fill, o'er-brimming all its measures,
    That dear ones near you stay.

'That hope attend you," but that, unforgetting,

    Some happy thoughts you hold

Of one who gladly, and past all regretting,

    His fairy gift has told.

# LOVE'S DEATH.

Oh ! say that this is not love's death ;

How could I live, were life's own breath—

   The breath of love—for ever flown ?

Then say it lives, though, like some fire,

It gives one flash, but to expire,

   And all the world is darker grown.

      Then say that this is not love's death,

      Its last expiring, silent breath.

My love is like the aloe's bloom,

It flowers but once, then seeks a tomb ;

   Like mortal love, its all is spent ;

Or like the dying swan's refrain,

So perfect, yet ne'er heard again,

   Till with the angels' music blent.

Then, then recall this fleeting breath,—

Say, are these broken hopes love's death ?


My life was all mine own ; you came,

And life remained, but not the same—

It took the hue of paradise :

Your smile the soul within me stirred,

Your laugh more sweet than woodland bird,

My love—a willing sacrifice.

Oh ! then how can this be the death

Of love all fresh with morning's breath


Another stirs the chords I fain

Would waken to love's breath again,

His hand the master touch supplied ;

And yet I crave for love one hour,

The last and most despairing power,

An idol fallen in its pride.

Then  snap  not  chords  which  are  love's

breath,

But tear the living thing from death.


But if, beloved, all must go

And fade as sunbeams melt the snow ;

I leave this last sad song to tell,

That though my love as madness burned,

Consuming fire and unreturned—

I love thee, dear—ah me ! too well.

But say that this is not love's death,

Its last expiring, silent breath.

# BURIED.

SHALL I tell the story
Of tenderest glory,—
   The love that was perfect and best ;
In the old churchyard,
With its white tombs starred,
   I have laid it away at rest.

In the sun's last wave
We stood by the grave
   Of some one whose story we guessed ;
In the soft spring weather,
With hands clasped together,
   We pitied them there in their rest.

And the wild flowers sweet

That grew round our feet

    As we dreamed out the sweet old dream,

Seemed to know of our love;

And the blue sky above

    Delayed long the sun's last gleam.


Oh! time without measure,

So laden with treasure,

    The joys that are now long ago;

Oh! the days that have fled,

And the dream that is dead,

    With a requiem chanted of woe!


And then, when at last

The sun's light had passed

    Once more to its shadowy home,

We rose with a sigh

That the days must die,

    And loitered away in the gloam.


But love's best token,

Its faith, was broken,

    And never again can I stray

In the starry night,

With a heart as light

    As the lark's, at the dawn of day.


Yet, ah me ! the love

That came from above,

    Filling my life with its glory ;

With the old dream gone,

I must journey on,—

    I have buried the sweet old story.

And many who smile

Remember the while

   A love that was perfect and best ;

In some old churchyard,

With its white tombs starred,

   Like me, they have lain it at rest.

# DREAMING.

THE tents are white on the battle-field,
　　But the dreamer sits apart,
And, as she dreams in twilight hour,
　　She speaketh to her heart.

"Oh ! say," she cries, "is it better to fight,
　　And climb, with failing breath,
The difficult hills which tend, we know,
　　To the silent land of Death ?

"Or better to rest, as I rest to-night,
　　In the peace of a neutral world—
To glide, like a phantom, at last to the grave,
　　With never a flag unfurled ? "

"Oh ! better to fight and die with a smile ;

   Oh ! better to have and to give,

For Death may be well at the close of the day,

   But the glory of Life is to live."

# TAKE UP THY LIFE.

Take up thy life as thou feelest, and not by a
written law ;

Nor measure thy sins or thy virtues by those that
have gone before.

Take up thy life as thou knowest, pointing for ever
to right,

As a mariner trusts to his compass, out on the
stormiest night.

Not from the words of the preacher, and not from
the lips of the sage ;

But the feelings that have been and will be for
ever an unwritten page ;

Creeds now adhered to may perish, old laws may

pass from our sight,

But we know well the soul's truest feeling is point-

ing for ever to right.

# PART II.

## Poems

BY

CYRIL HAVILAND.

'97

# GOD-NATURE.

God-Nature! to thee is my song; I kneel at thy
altar and worship.

Thy solitudes speaking with love, where all find
sweet sympathy ever;

Where the sad meet comfort and peace, and the
happy feel the more joyous,—

For thy presence never intrudes, but mirrors the
mood of the seeker,—

I offer my song unto thee; at thy feet I pour out
my worship.

God-Nature! receive thou my heart: it leaps to thy
pictures and fancies,—

To the song of the birds in the trees, to butterflies
flitting and poising,

To the circling leaves as they fall, to the hum of
    bees in the flowers,

To ferns as they tenderly grow, covering the dead,
    broken branches

Storm-hurled from their glory on high, where they
    kissed the rays of the Morning.

.

The ocean afar sings of thee, and the tree-tops
    answer far inland ;

The rough, rugged outlines of Earth,—as they edge
    the distant horizon

And stand back against the red sky, like silhou-
    ettes sharp in the sunset,—

Take up the grand chorus of love, and my heart
    leaps forth in its struggle

To join in the psalms that are sung ; but it fain
    would listen in wonder.

Thy freedom is fraught with a calm and soft, holy
  feeling of fitness.

Nothing jars the tenderest sense ; the laugh of the
  jackass above me

Melts in with the chatter of birds, as they pick the
  young, tinted gum-leaves ;

And the trickling water afar, as it falls o'er rocks
  in the gullies,

But blends like a symphony sweet with the clear,
  shrill note of the bell-bird.


Thy every shadow and shape is but of man's life a
  reflection ;

As the young trees grow gnarled and grey with
  fighting the force of the tempest,

So child-life grows wrinkled and worn with battling
  life's trials and troubles.

As the sea in its ceaseless surge beats to sand the

    cliffs of hard granite,

So Time, with his swift, silent step, breaks down

    the stout hearts of the strongest.


The limitless space of clear air, whose depth gives

    the sky its bright blueness,

In which a white cloud swiftly sails—its tips with

    warm sunshine made snowy

And its valleys darkened with shade,—as a life that

    knew not of sorrow,

Till there came some silver-edged grief,—the death

    of some loving companion,—

And the cloud of sorrow is tipped with sunshine of

    hope for the future.


The violets wild, white and blue, that under dark

    turpentines cluster,

Nod with the grass to the breeze, and gum-
    blossoms shake down their petals,

While I stand enwrapped in thy love, bidding
    farewell to the sunset

As the daylight softs into night, and the stars, like
    guardian angels,

Whisper to me as I listen, " Thou, too, art part of
    God-Nature."

# THE JENOLAN CAVES.

HERE swept the surgings of an ancient sea,
    And on each foamy crest
    The white-plumed gulls found rest,
While ocean flowers of all the hues that be
    Bent their long leafy lace,
    In ever-changing grace,
In the dark recesses of that tossing sea.

Beneath the surface of that tossing sea
The coral polyp built its fragile house,
Gathering with its sweeping tentacles
The minute atoms that the inland rain
Had washed from off the neighb'ring mountain
    side.

Here reared the polyps many busy homes—

A living colony of tinted fringe

For ever watchful, as around it swept,

Seizing on that it touched, and by degrees

Transforming it to wall or nourishment—

Until, as ages passed and ages came,

There grew, beneath the tides that rose and fell,

A wall whose length made many, many miles,

And in whose perforated, terraced sides,

Lived countless creatures, hydra-like in shape

Each one a helpless, soft, defenceless thing

That man could crush—ay, almost with a breath—

And yet whose work, from a united band,

Had raised a wall could ocean storms withstand.


Nature, with giant strength, at times bursts forth,

　　Then trembles earth and quakes to hear her

　　　　call ;

Like thundering noises in that frozen north,

    When great ice-mountains crack and crushing

        fall—

Elsewhere flash lightnings in the angry cloud,

    Tempestuous waves fling on the passive sand;

The whole earth shakes in anguish, and a shroud

    Of sea sweeps over newly sunken land.


The work of ages, in a moment sunk

Too deep for life, and all that myriad host

Lay slain and strewn, scattered by storm and sea.

Each home, that but just now was filled with life,

Into a tomb had turned, each worker dead

That built itself so lovely an abode ;

All folded is that tinted, living fringe

For ever.   A few short hours have made

A cemetery, where were happy homes.

Now may the ages pass, no living arms

Shall stop the sea-dust settling on those graves ;—

But day by day, and years and centuries,—

As ancient Egypt's Sphinx was covered in,

As crumbling rocks and Time's decaying dust

Have covered cities of this changing world,—

So have these cities, once· so full of life,

Been heaped high over with the years' decay,

Until in silence, by Time's work alone,

The erstwhile living homes have changed to

    stone.


Once more the lightnings thundered,

Once more the hills were sundered,

Once more the ocean heaved, and in its foamy

    fleeting

The rocks arose and towered,

The sea was overpowered,

Hurled from its citadel, yet inch by inch retreating.


That, which was sea-born, now by Nature's force

Was lifted heavenward, out beyond the waves;

And sun and cloud, in turn so favouring it,

Ere many years, had clothed it with a dress

Of ferns and flowers and trees, and beauteous

    birds

Found places safe wherein to sing and build.

In course of ages, then, the gentle rains

Had filtered through the soil, and in the cracks

And crannies of that ancient coral rock

Found temporary rest, until again,

In further travels where the stone had gaped,

Some tiny streams had trickled out their way,

Melting such parts as water could dissolve,

And carving chambers full of tracery;

Until like liquid glass a dewdrop hung

Half-hesitating,—as a maiden might,—

To seek the wonder of an unknown step,

And launch itself in space.

              Yet comes one more,

And others follow, crowding from behind,

Until, by force it could not well withstand,

One half the dewdrop fell, and by its fall

Gave birth to one such stalagmitic form,

Whose growth each sister drop has added to.

The other half looked downward from above,

A stalactite of beauty and of grace;

And as each drop of glistening dew took rest

And fell, but to be caught by that below,

So grew those alabastrine gems, until

The two were met in one, and parted drops

Were joined again in one delightful whole.

So sea-born rocks, cast high 'mid mountain land,

Have furnished sculptures for no human hand.


Perpetual night reigns here,—no sun nor star

   E'er shed a ray to lighten up the gloom ;

   These stalactites are headstones in the tomb

      Time built in the afar.


Here stands a monument of purest white,

   Begun in ages that have long since died,—

   Ere the first Pharaoh won his brownéd

    bride,—

      Its youth had seen that sight.


In after ages, when this earthly ball

Had spun ten thousand times around the sun,

Amidst the multitudes of life, came I,

A unit in the millions that had breath

Upon the world's broad surface, and mine eyes

Were turned in wonder upon Nature's art;

It seemed to me a realistic dream,—

A dream, I feared, would melt into my sleep.

'Twas thus—

      I stood within the bosom of the earth

Where Father Time had played with sculptor's

    tools,

And in his leisure moments, here and there,

Had chiselled out quaint alabastrine forms.

Around me, here, hung pendent from the roof,

A thousand spears, studded with rarest gems,

That glittered and reflected back the light

From the small glimm'ring taper that I held,

Until it seemed as if ten thousand stars

Were glistening in a miniature sky;

About me, set upon the marbled floor,

Were other spears that reached their serried points

Toward the threatening armament above ;

While here and there a warrior clad in white,—

And frosted over with a silver sheen

Surpassing all man's best magnificence,—

Towered his giant form above the rest ;

Upon the walls each warrior's robes hung down,

All set with jewels of the rarest hues.


While yet I stood, as one in wonder lost,

A voice spoke silent words within my soul :—

" Five thousand years have passed since that small
        point,

That now stands but a hand's-breadth high, was
        not ;

Ten thousand years winging their onward course

Have added but a span unto this form,

And yet it seems but yesterday to me

That have been here for ever and for aye."

I saw 'twas Father Time himself who spoke,

And bowed my head in deep and holy thought;

While over the awed surface of my mind

A wondrous thought came stealing silently,—

That here in darkness was this beauty wrought,

And since 'twas formed had never to this day

Been kissed by breeze, nor sunned by golden ray.

I turned, and wandered on with falt'ring step,

Under high arches, into caverns deep,

Where lovely forms of whitest marble stood

Like snowy fretwork gates to depths of dark.

Here reared a shape in alabaster pure,

Formed like a mother, with her babe enwrapped

In shielding arms, while with one foot she stept,

Half hoping, and yet half afraid to flee ;

And so had turned to stone.

Nature never

Had made before so beauteous a thing.

A few steps more, and at my feet what seemed

A moving, busy, restless, crushing crowd

Of pigmies rose to view, while looking down

Stood I, a giant from some other world.

A puny city this,

Where gath'ring crowds, as though expectant, wait

To hear important news.    In miniature

It calls to mind the cities of our earth,

Where men and women, each intent with haste,

Go hurrying forth with self-important speed

That sinks itself to insignificance

By next day's death.

But picture yet again :

Mark how the walls divide this city through,

With crystal ramparts flanked, a lifelike view

Of our own world, where walls of party strife

Divide and subdivide our human life.


Adown a passage tortuous and dark,—

A corridor of curious shapes and forms,

Which words could not describe,—I went alone,

And thought how wondrous strange it was that I,

A being of these days, should thus intrude

Upon the secret caverns of the past ;—

For, stooping down, I picked from out the rock

A shell, whose inmate once had ocean space

To move and live—a shell whose fossilled tongue

Could speak of ages yet unknown to man,

When monsters roamed the earth in search of food.

And as my self thus met the sacred past,

I almost stopped my sacrilegious feet,

When suddenly upon my view there burst ·

A sight that made me pause in thought profound,

To marvel at the wonders grouped around.


It seemed :—

　　　　Here dwelt a giant sculptor,

Whose massive tools no ordinary man

Has ever used, and from the giant rocks

He carved grotesque impossibilities.

'Twas here he toiled and slowly sculptured forth

Perfect suggestions, not realities ;

Fancies that had no earthly counterpart,

And then, alarmed at these strange fantasies,

In haste had fled and left them as they were,

Uncouth, unfinished, beautiful, complete.

Once more I onward moved, until beneath

I saw reflected from my taper's light

The stilly surface of a shimm'ring stream ;

A river that awhile had sought repose

From the too-glaring light of sun and day.


In silence 'neath the breast of Mother Earth

Crept on those hidden waters in the dark,

Carving a pathway for the sinuous stream

'Neath rocks of brown o'erhanging ruggedness,

Or snowy stalactites of various shapes,

Until they leapt again into the light,

And chased the sunbeams down the mountain

    height.


Let me, too, follow to the outer world,

Where in some spot, alone, 'mid graceful ferns,

I yet may think of Nature's giant work,—

The labour of the ages,—whose small shell
Speaks from the past, a wondrous tale to tell.


Oh ! thou great patient Architect, whose plan
Works on for ever,—what to thee is man ?
Each century thy perfect work shall see,
Yet never finished shall thy labours be.


Oh ! Time, thou writest well on marbled page
   A story wonderful of bygone days ;
For in that book we read of long past age,
Of work and toil that would have vexed a sage
   To plan, but thou hast very perfect ways.
Thy spoiling wrecks, thou accident, are part
Of that great scheme, where Nature teaches Art.


Each finger-mark, oh ! Time so plainly shows
   How vast the labour and how long the toil ;

For every rock bears marks of natal throes,

And leaf by leaf in Nature's volume glows

   With pencillings that ages may not spoil.

What book so grand, what page so marks each day,

And makes a witness even of decay?

# AN AUSTRALIAN MORNING.

WHOE'ER at morning greets the rising sun,

    And marks the dawning of the light of day —

Watching the mountain-tops tint one by one,

    And valley shadows swiftly melt away ;

        He sees the harmonies of Nature rise,

        Rose russets melting into azure skies.

He sees the robe of night so softly shed

    That day comes creeping unawares o'er all ;

The birds awake, and songs of praise o'erhead

    Mingle with ripplings from each tiny fall ;

        From Nature's inmost soul an anthem sways,

        From Earth vibrating on morn's golden rays.

# AN AUSTRALIAN EVENING.

SILENTLY and softly fell the evening shadows,
   We knew the day would soon be dead and past;
The cows were turning homewards from the
      meadows,
   And twilight seemed too beautiful to last.

Forth, through the fretwork of the tree-tops came
      a glory,
   Slowly the sun sank in the radiant west,
Adding to time one day, to life one story,
   Making in toil another hour of rest.

Gently across the water shone a path, so golden,
   It pointed upward like a holy wand,

Where time is not, days neither new nor olden,
    And all are happy in one loving bond.

Peace reigned supreme, the silvery star-worlds
      shining,
    Came one by one until the sky was bright ;
And dancing wavelets, all the sea entwining
    In chains, reflected from the gems of night.

The cricket chirped his lullaby around us,
    Soothing the birds, who long had gone to rest ;
So well has Nature with her sweetness bound us,
    That all things prove our Father's love is best.

WESTWARD the sun is sinking in a glorious golden
    lake,
    And far outspread from north to south, a fiery
        banner flies,
Tipping the clouds with rosy hues, while shape by
    shape they take,
    As silently, by zephyrs fanned, they cross the
        depthless skies

Gone is the sun,—Earth's gilded edge in memory
    keeps a trace ;—
    The clouds are being hidden by the darkness of
        the night ;

225                    Q

And one by one the stars peep forth, as though
they feared to face

The king of day, whose glory has but faded from
our sight.

Softly the air is stirring, and the rustling tree-tops
sing,

Keeping time to Nature's music, an evensong of
peace ;

And richly jewelled, far and wide, the sky is glittering

With stars, that, as night older grows, in number
fast increase.

Then the scent of gum-trees mingles with that of
flowers sweet,

And the night seems still and sacred, wrapped in
a holy dream ;

And all things tend to peace and love—would time

were not so fleet ;

Yet, in a night so beautiful, Earth has one happy

gleam.

# AUSTRALIAN WOODS.

Oh, peaceful woods, I woo your loneliness,
  Your shaded walks and quiet, resting nooks,
Where Nature breathes, in all her happiness,
    "Sermons in stones, and books in running
      brooks,"
Where grow fresh ferns in all their loveliness,
  Or violets peep, as some shy maiden looks.

The gleams of sun that seem in joyfulness
  To shine between the stems of storm-worn trees,
That light the distant scene with cheerfulness,
  And lend a radiance to the rustling breeze,

As in the rays it shakes in playfulness

    The lustrous leaves, in graceful ecstasies;

The wattle trees that in their comeliness

    Dress in the golden robe of early spring ;

The pendent vines that hang in loftiness,

    Adorning branches, where the finches sing,

And covering the many marks of hoariness

    Left by cold winter, when he last took wing ;

The butterflies that flit in laziness

    From flower to flower, and sip the honey sweet,

The lizard as he lies all motionless

    In the warm sunshine, basking in its heat—

All these endow the woods with holiness,

    That in my walks my heart so loves to greet.

# THROUGH THE TREES.

A WINDING path, amid a grassy lawn,
  And flowers and trees, in beauty growing there,
The river at my feet—a peaceful dawn ;
  All nature makes my picture passing fair.

So calm the water, that, as silvered glass,
  Reflections there are seen of every stone,
And boats are doubled, as they swiftly pass,
  And Nature sits upon a pictured throne.

# EVENING IN PORT JACKSON.

LIKE fire, the rays of the setting sun emblaze the
    crested sea,
    While a white-sailed ship steals silently upon the
    golden way,
And between the headlands grey gulls skim the
    foam-tipped waves in glee,
    As if they knew the night would close their
    careless evening play.

At the harbour gates the dark old cliffs uprear
    their roughened sides,
    And deep in the shadow sleep the bays, wrapped
    in the cloak of night ;

While the silvery sand beaches brightly shine,
where changing tides
  Have ebbed and flowed for centuries, washing
  their edges white.

On the barrier rocks, like crystals, the misty, wave-
thrown spray
  Of broken seas is falling, in a shower of snowy
  rain ;
And there gleams a rainbow glory as it meets a
parting ray
  From the setting sun, a last farewell, that wel-
  comes it again.

Then as night her starry mantle draws in silence
o'er each bay,
  And deeper shadows far outstretching darken
  the sea's rough breast,

Which 'neath rocky ledges sobs a soft, sad good-bye
  to the day,
  The far mountains stand like silhouettes against
  the fading west.

All now is peace, and the city's strife is hushed,
  and mortals sleep,
  And the waves in their deep surgings seem to
  mark the dreamy sea,
And tired Nature resting waits till the blush of
  dawn shall creep
  And wake her with a kiss of love on each
  mountain, rock, and tree.

# SUNSET.

When my boat sets sail to that golden west,
    And my soul is borne away;
When after life's labour I seek my rest—
    The close of my worldly day—
Then the tints and gleams of those glorious streams
    That flow from the setting sun,
Shall light to its goal that freight of a soul,
    For then shall my day be done.

When my death-hour comes, let it be like this:
    A glory of golden hue,

When the magnified sun just seems to kiss

    The clouds that float in the blue.

When the sky in the west is in glory dressed,

    And the clouds seem a sacred shore,

Let my soul then float, in its beautiful boat,

    To the Ocean of Evermore.

# MOONRISE AT COOGEE.

I STOOD upon the rocks one moonlight night ;
   The cares of earth outblotted by the scene
That stretched forth from my feet, and held my
      sight
Bound with the bonds of wonder and delight,
   For here man's reckless hand had never been.

The moon just risen shed a cold, white dawn,
   That frosted Ocean's edge and dimmed each
      star ;
A picture of that first pale mother-morn
That with warm love has since o'er hill-tops borne
   Those ruddy tints that mark day's birth afar.

Outstretched the sea, like some dark giant tossed,

    Writhing in chains that bound it in their might ;

And threat'ning waves with curly crests embossed,

Were with bright threads of silver edging crossed—

    A fretwork filagree of living light.

And o'er my soul that solemn feeling crept,

    When holier thought encounters God-like plan ;

As Ocean's grand eternal anthem swept,

And from the Universe a refrain leapt—

    " How great is Nature, and how small is man !"

# A FRAGMENT.

THE stars shine down upon me as I gaze into the
  sky,

The clouds skim lightly o'er the moon, and swiftly
  hurry by,

The chirping cricket greets me as I linger near the
  gate,

Of days long buried, thinking sadly, lonely there I
  wait,

And as I search into that space, and see those
  worlds so bright,

Softly to my heart I whisper, "God watches here
  to-night."

# THE DEATH OF THE DAYS.

To-DAY is born of yesterday, and yesterday is past
    And buried in that sepulchre of which Time
        holds the key;
The future opens hour by hour, and all things age
      so fast
    That the child has grown to manhood ere he
        knows what 'tis to be.
And yet no requiem is sung, no bell is tolled to
      mark
    The sun's last ray reflected from some silent
        passing cloud.

And with the yesterdays now gone, as twilight
   deeps to dark,
  Another day is laid away, wrapped in a golden
   shroud.

# LIFE'S SNOW.

Yonder she sits, doubled with age, and grey
    Are the locks that once were bright and brown;
Wrinkled and careworn is her face to-day,
    Yet once her beauty won her great renown.
Eighty swift summers have the timeworn oaks
    Spread forth their leaves, till autumn gave her
      voice;
Eighty white winters in their snow-wrapped cloaks
    Have come, till spring has bid earth's heart
      rejoice;
Eighty long years has she life's pathway stept,
    And Death has looked, and smiling passed her
      by,

While friends and playmates to his arms have
    crept
  To sleep, too tired to stop, too glad to die ;
Yet she, so old and aged and bent with care,
Was once, long years ago, both young and fair.

# YOU AND I.

Do we know it as we should,

    You and I,

That through Life's mist-tangled wood

    Draweth nigh

The Angel Death, who never

    Passeth by ?


Sure as sunset follows day,

    You and I

Will feel the Angel's touch, nor stay

    Asking " Why ? "

Only knowing, as we know,

    All must die.

# ACROSS THE RIVER.

THE earth is bright and glad with flowers,
　　All laden is the air with scent ;
But, day by day the fleeting hours
　　Pass on to Time's high monument.

Life and true love are joyous things,—
　　Though sadness sometimes casts a shade,
Though swift are sorrow's gloom-tipped wings,
　　For us the lovely earth was made.

The free and happy birds that fill
　　The peaceful forests with their song,
Join in the music of the rill
　　That chants its fountained course along.

Then let us live and happy be ;

   The earth is all with gladness rife,

And all things are for you and me ;

   So let us live a joyous life.


\*     \*     \*     \*


What now is this that comes between

   My sight, and stops my struggling breath ?

Tell me, why fades earth's lovely scene ?

   Tell me, is this the tyrant Death ?


\*     \*     \*     \*


I wake !  Methought I slept the sleep

   When happy life shall cease its breath ;

And o'er my senses seemed to creep

   The cold and chilliness of death.

Can this be true? I live once more;

Earth's troubles past—its joy and strife.

Death is the opening of the door,

And Life is one eternal Life.

# A VOICE FROM THE WESTERN HILLS.

God's works are grand—each hill and dell,
   Each forest clothed with bush and tree,
And rushing torrents nobly tell
   Of wisdom, might, and majesty ;
The sweeping storm, the sighing wind,
   The birds that chant their songs of praise,
All speak of one most wondrous mind,
   Whom the whole universe obeys.

I stood on high, and looked around ;
   I saw the mountains far away,

I saw their peaks, in snow robes bound,

    Reflect the sun's all-glorious ray—

I watched the white mist roll aside,

    The veil of night from nature **drawn**—

As doth a pretty blushing bride,

    So peeped the earth that sunny **morn**.


And I, an atom on this earth,

    Bowed down my head in holy thought,

That all for man such **scenes** had **birth**,

    That all for man such **work** was wrought.

What then am I, when dangers **near**

    Assail me round on every hand ?

Alone, with every doubt and fear,

    Alone, I can no moment **stand** ;—


But in the God who fashioned man—

    The Ruler of th' unmeasured space,

Whose love the unknown worlds doth span,

    I, trustfully, still run my race !

And when my sought-for goal is won,

    And I in His pure presence live,

I cannot give Him but His own, —

    My thanks were never mine to give.

# WOODLAND THOUGHTS.

DEEP in the shady haunts of ferns I wandered,
 Thinking on life, its gladness and its grief;
And as I Nature's speaking silence pondered,
 Circling there fell from high a broken leaf.

A leaf, a life,—the bud and then the flower,
 The leaflet young and tender as a child,—
Browned, hardened, worn by every passing hour,
 Broken and dead, tossed by each whirlwind
  wild.

The grove I stood in, by its mantle darkened,
 Rich in the lessons that I fain would learn;—

Each tree and fern spoke thoughts to which I
hearkened,

Fresh visions waited me at every turn.

The very shade itself portrayed the mortal,

The man whose life was sorrowful indeed ;

And then a sunny ray, through some leaf portal,

Pictured a hope,—a friend in time of need.

Above the shade the treetops tall and bending,

Tinged with a glory of the life to be,

Each to the other grace and radiance lending,—

All peace and love beyond earth's cares I see.

# THE POOL.

I stood upon the margin of a pool,
　　And watched the orange-tinted hornet drink ;
Or noted butterflies, that in the cool
　　Waited awhile upon the mossy brink.

The stilly surface mirrored forth the sky
　　That gave no limits to the cloudless sphere ;
And on the ground beneath, where pebbles lie,
　　Prismatic sun-rays glittered bright and clear.

Some floating leaves here found a resting-place,
　　Casting their outlines on the depths below ;
And their dark shadows wove a golden lace,
　　Edged with the glory of a rainbow's glow.

Here the grey spider spun a web so fine

    From bank to bank, from flower to arching

        frond,

All round the pool in one unbroken line,

    Chaining much beauty in a fairy bond.

# ON THE HAWKESBURY.

THE sun sinks slowly in the west,

The ripples lull themselves to **rest** ;

    The red, reflected sky

**Inflames the river, tints the trees,**

**While softly sobs the evening breeze,**

    Because the day **must die.**

The fiery clouds mild **tones assume,**

The stars begin night **to illume ;**

    They glisten everywhere ;

**And** pleasant thoughts **our minds imbue,**

**As night gives all a softer hue ;**

    For peace **supreme is there.**

Between the banks we gently glide

Upon our way.   On either side

    The trees' dark shade is seen.

While Venus sheds a silvery ray,

The lesser stars dot o'er our way,

    And we glide on between.

# THE SEASONS.

How beautiful the earth is when the spring

    Clothes with its newborn tints the timeworn

    trees ;

When Nature smiles on man, and seems to sing

    Rejoicings, borne upon each passing breeze !

How glorious the hills in summer look,

    When radiant gleams light up more sombre

    shades !

Then would I choose me some retirèd nook,

    And watch each colour as it slowly fades.

How fairy-like in autumn is the view,

    When from the trees the tinted leaves fall fast,

And the sun shines in glory on each hue,—

    Reflections of a life that now is past !

How calm and still in winter Nature's sleep,

    When snowy hillocks mark the furrowed ground,

And frozen tears the dripping streamlet keep,—

    Waiting unrest,—the echoes to resound !

# A SUMMER STORM.

THE clouds rise up, the sky grows dark
  That but just now was bright and clear ;
The lightning flashes, and now, hark !
  The thunder rolls afar, anear.

Down pours the rain, and tiny rills
  Run races on the window-pane ;
A vivid flash comes o'er the hills,
  A rumble, and 'tis gone again.

Thunder and lightning everywhere,
  The day seems turning into night ;
A break comes in the clouds, and there
  As soon again 'tis clear and bright.

# AUSTRALIA.

SEE here the beauteous form of a fair maid,

   As from her veil—sweet Nature's robe of

     green—

She steps, half hoping and yet half afraid,

   From ferns and flowers, where her young life

     has been.

When at her birth the mighty sea gave way,

   And she, the child of promise, rose on high,

Her lap was filled with blessings, and the day

   Shone joyously, the babe to beautify.

\*　　\*　　\*　　\*

A land of promise for the sons of toil,

Where Nature yet should yield her lavish spoil.

So dawned the century with golden rays,

Lighting Australia's steps to nobler ways.

# LAND OF THE SUNNY SOUTH.

AN AUSTRALIAN NATIONAL ANTHEM DEDICATED

TO THE PEOPLE OF NEW SOUTH WALES.

*(Set to music by Signor Giorza, and sung at the Opening of the
International Exhibition, Sydney, 1879.)*

LAND of the Sunny South, all hail !

God prosper thee in peace,

And may thy riches never fail,

Thy flocks and herds increase.

Advance, Australia ! onwards press,

Thy children give thee love,

And pray that God will ever bless

Thy progress from above.

CHORUS.

God bless thee and cherish thee,

Australia ! sunny land,

And keep thee in prosperity

With blessings from His hand.

Our God hath prospered thee in wealth,

With mines of untold gold ;

Thy soil abounds in life and health,

In riches manifold.

Then let us praise His holy name

For this our native land,

For all thy welfare doth proclaim

The glory of His hand.

Long may'st thou prosper on and thrive,

    And ever gain renown ;

And may thy children always strive

    To win thee vict'ry's crown.

We love thee, bright Australia dear,

    Land of the fruitful vine ;

We pray that God be ever near

    To watch o'er thee and thine.

# KISSES.

Oh, love with coral lips,

Where kisses dwell,

Let me but touch the tips

I love so well.

Let me but steal one kiss

From out thy wealth ;

Thou, sleeping, shalt not miss

One gained by stealth.

And if thou wakest, dear,

Take one from me ;

Lips are for kissing, dear,

Where'er love be.

Kissing and loving, sweet,

All our lives through ;

So, our lips softly meet,—

Thus kiss I you.

# LOVE THOUGHTS.

THOUGH many miles between us lie, sweetheart
    mine,
  And sunny slopes may hide thee from my sight ;
Yet, 'cross the space my love-thoughts fly, sweet-
    heart mine,
    O'er leaping mountains in their instant flight.
      All chains must break and prison bars must
        part,
      Love-thoughts take wing and nestle to thy
        heart ;
      For space is nought, and love-thoughts quickly
        flee
      O'er rugged mountains or the crested sea, to
        thee,
            Sweetheart mine, only mine.

# A LOVE SONG.

Oh ! Morning, roseate with those glorious hues,
　　Sweet with a freshness, welcomed with the glee
　　Of birds, take kisses to my love from me,
And give them safely with thy purest dews,
　　To my belovèd who is o'er the sea.

Ye Noonday Zephyrs, balmy with the scent
　　Of fragrant flowers, quickly to her flee
With love-thoughts laden, all your sighings blent,
　　To my belovèd who is o'er the sea.

And Evening, thou bespangled hour of day,
　　When every brook is sparkled, list to me !
Canst thou, too, give me e'en a silvery ray
To bear my message, words of love to say
　　To my belovèd who is o'er the sea ?

# WHAT IS LOVE?

" WHAT is Love ? " sang forth the stream

   As it went rippling 'neath the trees ;

There fell from heaven a sunny gleam,

   And birds gave forth sweet melodies,—

           And that is Love.


" What is Love ? " so spoke a girl,

   As, pausing on the stream's green edge,

The breeze shook out each glossy curl—

   A youth appeared thro' yonder hedge,

           And she found Love.

" What is Love ? " a woman sighed—

There came to her a vision white,

And to her heart a spirit cried :

" I am an angel pure and bright,

And bring you Love."


" What is Love ? " sought a sad soul.

" Knowest thou aught, save but in name ? "

The whole earth shook from pole to pole—

From Nature's heart an answer came :

"Our God is Love."

# AN EPIGRAM.

Love is to be of all the rest

The dearest, sweetest, and the best;

That which of all else far above

Can only be expressed by Love.

# DO NOT FORGET.

When far away, oft let your mem'ry go

    Back to that southern land of depthless skies,

Where o'er the rocks the sun-kissed ripplets flow,

    And in blood-crimson clouds the daylight dies.

Think sometimes of the graceful ferns that bend

    O'er mossy covered spots with shelt'ring love ;—

Of the blue hills that in the distance blend

    The earth's faint limit with the sky above.

When far away, as fly the hast'ning hours,

    Let visions oft invade those thoughts of thine ;

Let pictures rise of glades o'erstrewn with flowers,

    Where daylight only fades that stars may shine.

Yes, I would have thee, both by night and day,

  Dream of the days that sped in these bright

  lands;

And in thy mem'ry, when thou art away,

  Keep one green spot for southern hearts and

  hands.

# TO A FRIEND.

GENTLY on the river we glide,

    The ripples singing 'neath the boat,

    And waterlilies by us float

As we row from side to side.

Clear is the day and blue the sky :

    On either hand the cliffs are seen,

    Climbing cloudwards,—and between,

In the boat, just you and I.

A year hence, when the ocean sways

    Between us both, and we no more

    Can ramble as we did of yore,

Oft will we think of bygone days.

# BLIND.

Blind? Yes; I am blind from my birth, blind
from the day I was born,—
Yet I know of the glories of earth, of the golden
gate of dawn,
Of the radiant tints of the flowers, of the blue of
sky and sea ;
Though so dark are my earth-life's hours, yet earth
has a book for me.

In the free, open forest I sit, and list to songs of
the breeze,
To the hum of the insects that flit, to anthems of
love in the trees ;

I am told that the grass is so green, and in each

    long yellow lance

Of the gay, golden, glistening sheen, bright butter-

    flies float and dance.


By the sonorous chant of the sea, on the rocks, I

    sit all day,

And in fancy,—though blind I may be,—I know

    how the long waves play ;

I can count to the turn of each wave, as their

    measured time they keep,

I can hear in the deep rocky cave their boom as

    in wrath they leap.


Oh ! all you that have nature and sight, what is

    earth and sky to you ?

Does the beauty of day or of night ever thrill your

    senses through ?

Do you ever look into that blue, and **watch clouds**

    **blown by the wind?**

Or are these things so common to you, 'tis you and

    not I am blind?


Yes; **your** eyes may be **open and free, but blind**

    your innermost sight ;

You see, and yet never see.   What **to you is day**

    or night ?

A time only of labour or rest—a tree **is nought but**

    **a tree ;**

**Could I choose which I thought** was **best—I'd**

    **choose to** be blind, **yet see.**

# TIME.

Swiftly flows life's stream,
  The goal is near;
And from a waking dream
  We leave all here.

To-morrow is to-day,
  To-day is done;
And weeks thus roll away,—
  Their course is run.

Mem'ries of hours long past
  Some pleasures give;
For though they died at last,—
  They, dying, live.

# TIME'S REASON.

I CAUGHT Time as he flew, and bade him say

Why with such speed he closed each happy day,

Yet with sad slowness lengthened those of grief,

As if he fain would linger o'er that leaf

Of Life's great volume, where, in shade or sun,

Each day a page is silently begun.

Quoth he, " Where Grief is, there I tarry long ;

My heart-strings echo to the saddened song ;

For in true Sympathy all things respond,—

In Nature's law each must obey this bond,—

Where Happiness triumphant reigns, I fly,

But Pity folds my wings at Sorrow's cry."

# CHILDHOOD.

I PEEPED into a nursery, where toys were strewn
about;
Where some pretty little children were running in
and out,
    Their cleanly frocks and faces, their little airs
and graces,
Quite charmed me into joining in each gleeful
laugh and shout,
    And I looked back on my childhood, my boyish
games and races,
And I thought of those who since have died, that
I am left without,

And my mind went **back to scenes** in **years that**

**now are far away.**

   **But** my solemn thoughts unspoken,

   Were by merry music **broken**

   Of their patter as they run,

   **And** their clatter o'er their fun,

  **Oh,** these baby men and women **of to-day** !


I passed **upon a** roadside, **where tins and** shells

  were piled—

**The toys of** some poor **little** folks, **whose happi-**

  **ness beguiled**

  **Their thoughts from tattered dresses, and tossed**

  and matted tresses,

**And my heart** was **turned to sorrow as** I **gazed**

  **upon each child ;**

  **And I stood and watched these children, in the**

  **innocence which blesses.**

Such as these, and those who riches have, but
are not thus exiled ;

A loving God provides for both ; He sees them
at their play.

And my thoughts, again unspoken,

Were by childish voices broken,

As they chatter o'er their fun,

And their patter as they run,

Oh, these baby men and women of to-day !

# DEATH OF A CHILD.

DEATH brings no fear ; for, far and wide,

All men have lived, and, living—died,

And calmly gone with fleeting breath,

Into thine arms, O Angel Death.


Death and I stood by a bed,

I on the one side near her head ;

Death on the other, waiting awhile,

Biding his time with a saddened smile.


I held out my arms and begged her sta

Death shook his head and whispered " Nay ;

Trouble and care are on this earth,

Nothing for her is here of worth."

I kissed her just as her soul took flight,

For the Angel Death took her that night ;

And she had no fear, as she softly died,

When that Angel and I stood side by side.

# THE WATCH OF LIFE.

THE rosy tints o'er the eastern sky proclaim the
coming day,
The first hour in the watch of life thus pictured
by the dawn ;
And the bells of ships are striking, safe anchored
in the bay,
Marking with echoing voices another day is
born.

So in our life on earth,
The first hour of our watch, we hear,
Like spirit voices in our ear,

As a symbol of our birth,

    Two bells !

          Life's watch begun.

The sun has mounted to his height in a blue un-

    fathomed sky,

  The day is growing older, for life's zenith now

    is ours ;

And again we hear in fancy the ships fast sailing

    by,

Telling the watch is passing on, and Time has

    lost two hours.

    For we have reached an age

      When life is always at its best ;

      Soon must our earthly body rest.

    Hark ! as we turn the page,

        Four bells !   Four bells !

            On watch.

Draws the day so slowly to a close, and evening
    shadows grow
  In shapes that lengthen stealthily as daylight
    disappears ;
And we must be ageing also, for we falter as we
    go,
  Leaving a shadow, mem'ry, on the vast expanse
    of years.

        Old age, wrinkled and grey,
          Creeps slowly step by step so sure ;—
          Live truly, then, a life so pure,
        Ready to end the day—
          Six bells !   Six bells !   Six bells !

                              On watch.

The night has come at last, and in the still dark-
    ness, cold and drear,

Gleam forth the stars, so silvery, to point the

upward way ;

Our watch is over, and the bells are ringing sharp

and clear,

So hopefully that there will yet be born another

day.

Then shall our souls have fled

To spirit realms, where, free from strife,

Ringing, we hear at close of life—

When this soul's house is dead—

Eight bells ! Eight bells ! Eight bells ! Eight bells !

Life's watch is done.

# HYMN OF PRAISE.

LORD God, great Ruler of eternity,

    Before Thy grandeur humbly here we stand

And offer heartfelt thanks alone to Thee,

    Who with sweet peace has blessed our southern

      **land.**

We join our voices in the praises **poured**

From Nature's myriad throats to Thee, O **Lord !**

Thy glorious love is limitless as space,

    Encircling worlds or nourishing the flower ;

And we have known Thy holy, peaceful grace

    **In** which our land **has grown from birth to**

      **power.**

For this **we** offer all our praise to **Thee,**

Lord God, great Ruler of eternity.

288

www.ingramcontent.com/pod-product-compliance
Lightning Source LLC
Chambersburg PA
CBHW020855020726
47497CB00005B/1421